The Dinner Party

The Dinner Party

And Other Stories

Joshua Ferris

Little, Brown and Company

New York Boston London

Copyright © 2017 by Joshua Ferris

Little, Brown and Company
Hachette Book Group
1290 Avenue of the Americas, New York, NY 10104
littlebrown.com

First Edition: May 2017

Little, Brown and Company is a division of Hachette Book Group, Inc. The Little, Brown name and logo are trademarks of Hachette Book Group, Inc.

The publisher is not responsible for websites (or their content) that are not owned by the publisher.

The Hachette Speakers Bureau provides a wide range of authors for speaking events. To find out more, go to hachettespeakersbureau.com or call (866) 376-6591.

These stories originally appeared, sometimes in different form, or with different titles, in the following publications: "The Dinner Party," "The Valetudinarian," "The Pilot," "Fragments" (as "The Fragment"), "The Breeze," and "The Stepchild" (as "The Abandonment") in *The New Yorker;* "Ghost Town Choir" in *Prairie Schooner;* "A Night Out" in *Tin House;* "More Abandon" in *Best New American Voices;* "Life in the Heart of the Dead" in *Ploughshares;* and "A Fair Price" in *VICE.*

"The Valetudinarian" was reprinted in *The Best American Short Stories 2010.* "The Breeze" was reprinted in *The Best American Short Stories 2014.* "Ghost Town Choir" was reprinted in *New Stories from the South: The Year's Best 2007.*

ISBN 978-0-316-46595-3

LCCN 2016957621

10 9 8 7 6 5 4 3 2 1

LSC-C

Printed in the United States of America

For Cooper Ferris and Jim Shepard

Contents

The Dinner Party

The Dinner Party

On occasion, the two women went to lunch and she came home offended by some pettiness. And he would say, "Why do this to yourself?" He wanted to shield her from being hurt. He also wanted his wife and her friend to drift apart so that he never had to sit through another dinner party with the friend and her husband. But after a few months the rift would heal and the friendship return to good standing. He couldn't blame her. They went back a long way, and you got only so many good friends.

He leapt four hours ahead of the evening and saw, in future retrospect, that he could predict every gesture, every word. He walked back to the kitchen and stood with a new drink in front of the fridge, out of her way. "I can't do it," he said.

"Can't do what?"

The balls were up in the air: water coming to a boil on the stove, meat seasoned on the butcher block. She stood beside the sink dicing an onion. Other vegetables, bright and doomed, waited their turn on the counter. She stopped cutting long enough to lift her arm to her eyes in a tragic pose. Then she resumed, more tearfully. She wasn't drinking her wine.

"I can tell you everything that will happen from the moment they arrive to the little kiss on the cheek goodbye, and I just can't goddamn do it."

"You could stick your tongue down her throat instead of the kiss goodbye," she offered casually as she continued to dice. She was game, his wife. She spoke to him in bad taste freely, and he considered it one of her best qualities. "But then that would surprise her, I guess, not you."

"They come in," he said, "we take their coats. Everyone talks in a big hurry, as if we didn't have four long hours ahead of us. We self-medicate with alcohol. A lot of things are discussed, different issues. Everyone laughs a lot, but later no one can say what exactly was so witty. Compliments on the food. A couple of monologues. Then they start to yawn, we start to yawn. They say, 'We should think about leaving, huh?' and we politely look away, like they've just decided to take a crap on the dinner table. Everyone stands, one of us gets their coats, peppy goodbyes. We all say what a lovely evening, do it again soon, blah-blah-blah. And then they leave and we talk about them and they hit the streets and talk about us."

"What would make you happy?" she asked.

"A blow job."

"Let's wait until they get here for that," she said.

She slid her finger along the blade to free the clinging onion. He handed her her glass. "Drink your wine," he said. She took a sip. He left the kitchen.

He sat on the sofa and resumed reading his magazine. Then

he got up and returned to the kitchen and poured himself a new drink.

"That's another thing," he said. "Their big surprise. Even their goddamn surprises are predictable."

"You need to act surprised for their sake," she said.

"Wait for a little opening," he said, "a little silence, and then he'll say, he'll be very coy, he'll say, 'Why don't you tell them?' And she'll say, 'No, you,' and he'll say, 'No, you,' and then she'll say, 'Okay, okay, I'll tell them.' And we'll take in the news like we're genuinely surprised—like, holy shit, can you believe she's knocked up, someone run down for a Lotto ticket, someone tell Veuve Clicquot, that bastard will want to know. And that's just the worst, how predictable our response to their so-called news will be."

"Well, okay," she said. "When that happens, why don't you suggest they have an abortion?"

He chewed his ice and nodded. "That would shake things up, wouldn't it?"

"Tell them we can do it right here with a little Veuve Clicquot and one of the bedroom hangers."

"Delightful," he said. "I'm in."

The kitchen was small. He would have done better to remain in one of the other rooms, but he wanted to be with her. She was sautéing the garlic and the onion.

"He's okay," he said. "They're both okay. I'm just being a dick."

"We do this, what—at most, once or twice a year. I think you can handle it. And when they have the baby—"

"Oh, Christ."

"When they have the baby, we'll see even less of them."

"Holiday cards. Here's our little sun-chine. See our little sun-chine? Christ."

"You aren't the one who's going to have to go to the baby shower," she said.

"How much you wanna bet they buy a stroller?"

"A stroller?"

"Yeah, a stroller," he said. He put cheese on a cracker. "To cart the baby around in."

"I'm going to wager the odds of a stroller are high," she said. "But you, if you had a baby, there'd be no stroller, am I right? Because it would be oh so predictable to have a stroller, wouldn't it."

"I was thinking we could duct-tape the child," he said. "It would be cheaper."

"Like a BabyBjörn, but duct tape."

"Exactly."

"Would the baby face in or out?"

"If it was sleeping, in. Not sleeping, kind of kicking its feet, wanting to see the world, duct-tape it out, so it has a view."

"Allowing the child to be curious," she said. "Feeding its desire to marvel at this new experience called life."

"Something like that."

"The child must be so relieved that I'm barren," she said.

He left the kitchen. He stood in the living room with his drink, listening to the sounds of her cooking.

They should have invited Ben and Lauren, too, like last time. Ben and Lauren were more his friends. With Ben and Lauren there, time didn't move as it did in funeral parlors and in the midwestern churches of his youth. But she had wanted it just the four of them this time, probably so that they could more freely revel in their big news, and there was a limit to how many times he could say, unprompted, "Hey, should we invite Ben and Lauren?" At least he was doing Ben and Lauren a favor.

He returned to the kitchen. "When they come in," he said, "let's make them do a shot, both of them."

"A shot?"

"Of tequila."

"Her, too?"

"Both of them."

"To sort of . . . fortify the baby."

"We'll force them somehow," he said. "I'll figure it out."

"Better hurry," she said.

"All this talk of folic acid and prenatal vitamins. Give me a break. Do they think Attila the Hun got his daily dose of folic acid when he was in the womb? Napoleon?" She was going back and forth across the kitchen while he kept his drink close. "I could go on."

"George Washington," she said, "a Founding Father."

"See? I could go on. Moses."

"I don't think she's going to be willing to do a shot," she said.

"We trick her somehow. Tell her it's full of prenatal vitamins, and she shoots it down."

"Because she just graduated from the third grade," she said, "and she's blind and retarded."

"I'll think of something," he said.

He left the kitchen again. On his way back in, he said, "Okay, I've got it."

But the kitchen was empty. Her wedding ring and the one with the diamond were on the counter, where she always put them before starting to cook. The sink had filled with dishes. On the stove, the big pot and the smaller one unfurled steam into the rattling vent. The door under the sink hung open.

"Amy?" he said. No answer. Where was she? He turned and walked back the way he came, through the apartment, in the unlikely event that she had passed by without his noticing as he was lying on the sofa. Then he returned to the kitchen, to the animated appliances and stewing ingredients. She came in through the front door.

"Where'd you go?"

"Took the garbage out," she said.

"I would have done that."

"But you didn't," she said.

He had come into the kitchen with a whole new approach to the evening, but after she went missing, he was no longer in the mood to provoke her. Instead, he set his drink down and went up to her at the stove. He threaded his arms around her waist as she stirred one of the pots. Years earlier, they'd had a name for this hug. He couldn't remember what it was now. He kissed her neck, then the back of her hair. Her hair smelled of steam and shampoo and fake wildflowers. "What can I do?" he said.

"You can set the table," she said.

He set the table. Then he stood with his back to the refrigerator and with a new drink. "So I've figured it out," he resumed. "They bring the bottle of wine, right? We thank them, but we don't open it. We tuck it away in the kitchen. They never see it again. We start the evening. We don't ask them what they want to drink. Like it's just an oversight on our part. Because I know him. Even if she's not drinking because of the big news, he'll want a drink. I tell him we ran out. I tell him we'll open their wine at dinner. But then we don't. We just have water for the table. Then, in the middle of the meal—"

"No alcohol," she said. "You should work for al-Qaeda."

"—in the middle of the meal, I get up and go to the kitchen and I bring back a beer for myself. I open it at the table and take a long drink. What do you think?"

"Sounds promising."

"He says, 'Hey, got another one of those?' and I'm like, 'Oh, actually, this is the last one.' And then I kill it. Do you think they would leave?"

"Leave? No."

"Really? They wouldn't leave after that? Where the hell are they, anyway?"

"They might never come back, but no. They would not leave."

"You know, they're good people," he said. "Ultimately."

"She's my oldest friend," she said. "And he can be very funny."

"You're right, he can be funny."

Later, he came out of the bathroom just as the toilet was completing its roar. She was no longer in the kitchen. He took another cheese and cracker. He walked past the dressed table to the living room. She sat on the sofa reading the same magazine he had been reading. He stood in the middle of the room and held out his hands. "Where are they?"

"If there's one thing that's predictable," she said, "it's her running late."

"Sure, but it's going on forty-five minutes."

"They'll be eating some very cold appetizers."

"Have you cooked the meat?"

"Everything but."

She casually flipped through the magazine. There was no outrage or impatience. She seemed resigned to waiting as long as it took.

"You should maybe call her," he said.

"Isn't this what you wanted?" she asked. "Something unpredictable?"

She was on the phone, calling around. It was nine o'clock, and then it was ten, going on ten thirty. She tried to reach them a dozen times in a dozen different ways. She sent texts and emails. They didn't pick up and they didn't reply.

"Not when it interferes with dinner," he said.

"Nice," she said. "Magnanimous and humane."

"Listen, don't worry about those fucking drips," he said. "They have fallen asleep watching *Friends* on DVD, for which they have locked their doors and silenced their phones."

"Yes?" she said. She was speaking into the phone now. "Okay, thank you. Can you take my number just in case one of them comes in? Thank you." She left her name and number and hung up.

"Is it really possible," she said. She was dialing the next number. "Is it really possible that you care about no one but yourself?"

"I'm trying to be helpful."

"Your help isn't worth a good goddamn anymore," she said.

He didn't like to be reminded. He left the room. "Sure," she said to the phone. "I love to hold."

"Is this meat going bad?" he called out. He was in the kitchen. He had finished the cheese and crackers, the mini caprese salad she'd made with grape tomatoes, and the figs wrapped in bacon, caramelized with a homemade glaze. Now he was sitting on a bar stool eating a saucer of the mushroom risotto that was meant to go with the lamb, while staring at the meat on the butcher block. He had opened another bottle of wine. "Hey, babe, this meat? Should we do something with this meat?"

"Stick it up your ass," she said.

He stopped chewing. He looked with raised eyebrows at the two mustard-seasoned racks of lamb and thought how unpleasant it would be to insert one of their bony ribs into his butthole, but how much fun to walk out into the next room and moon her with a rack of lamb between his cheeks. "Stick it up my ass, huh," he said. "You know who should stick it up ... whose asses ... up whose asses it should be stuck up is, are your two friends of yours, their asses. They should stick it up their asses," he said.

Another hospital had no record, either, and again she left her name and number. She walked into the kitchen. "What are you muttering?"

"There are two racks there, one for each of their asses."

She put her fingertip on his forehead. "This isn't like them," she said, pushing his head back, "and you know it's not like them, and you're not being helpful." She released him, and he sprang back on the stool to an upright position.

"I'm sorry, am I supposed to be helpful?" he said. "Because I thought my help was no longer worth a good goddamn."

She left the room.

"Wait," he said. He dropped the risotto to the counter and got off the stool. "Hold on." He followed her through the dining room. "Obviously, I'm not saying—will you stop? will you listen to me, please?—that I don't want to be helpful. Will you please turn around and listen?" She stopped and turned. "They just got their dates wrong, is all," he said, "and tomorrow, when they call, they'll tell you how sorry they are. They had to turn their phones off during the late showing of *Kung Fu Panda* or something."

"So they went to see *Kung Fu Panda* tonight," she said.

"Something like that."

"My adult friends went to see *Kung Fu Panda* tonight, and they turned their phones off so they wouldn't ring during *Kung Fu Panda.* "

"Or," he said. "Or." He put up a finger. They were standing near the bedroom doorway. There was dim light coming from the dark room and he was suddenly irrationally afraid, as he had been as a child, that if anyone stepped inside, if she stepped inside, she would plummet to the center of the earth. He lowered his finger. "I'm sorry," he said. "I don't think they went to see *Kung Fu Panda.*"

"You do not think, period," she said.

She stepped inside the bedroom. She did not plummet down but floated across the murk into the bathroom. She waited until the door was shut before switching on the light.

He sat on the kitchen floor for thirty minutes. Then he said, "Hey!" He got no response. He stood and went into the bedroom.

He found her in bed. She was in her pajamas. She was propped up against the headboard, reading a book in the lamplight. "What are you doing?"

"Going to bed."

"The meat is still on the counter," he said. "There's food everywhere. Are we just going to let it go to waste? And aren't you worried about your friends?"

"I'm not hungry," she said.

"Should you really be reading a book right now?"

"What else would you suggest I do?"

"I don't know. Go over to their apartment? See if they're there?"

"I need to wait here in case I get a call from a hospital, or in case they show up."

He sat down on the bed. He put his head in his hands. He heard the slow turn of one page after another, and then, deeper in the ears, the squishy beat of his sobering heart.

"Well," he said, looking up. "Would you like me to go over there?"

"What are you going to do about it, big man? Man of steel? Gonna get inside the Absolutmobile and go find the big danger?"

He stared at her.

"It's too bad we can't have children," she said. "If she was ever abducted, what better daddy to go and save her?"

"Her? Is that right? Is it a her?"

"I guess it would be important for you to have a boy, wouldn't it? So you could pass along all these masculine skills of yours. All your big-man powers."

He stood up from the bed.

"Do you want me to go over there or not?"

He had been to their apartment a handful of times, but never with so many people in it. It was a sizable apartment with a quirky floor plan and a proliferation of rooms that seemed to spool out one after another. He stepped inside and saw the first of the bedrooms pulsing with a lot of carefully curated candlelight. He saw silhouettes of people there and more in the room to his right. People were coming and going from the kitchen, some louder than others. He did not recognize the man who had opened the door for him.

"Is there a party going on?" he asked.

"Are you a neighbor?"

"Old friend."

"There's beer in the fridge," the man said. He closed the door and turned back to his conversation.

The noisy talk was now crisper than it had been in the hall outside, where he had first picked up on its underwater strains and thought it must be coming from some other apartment. He hesitated before finally drifting down the small corridor to the kitchen. Here, too, the light was dim. More votives cast shadows against the chrome appliances and the ceiling-mounted pots and pans and all the people standing in clusters against the black marble counter. Someone reached into the fridge. The bright, telescoping light broke the ambience, and the door falling shut just as quickly restored it. "The last one of those, you bastard?" someone said. The one addressed mimicked smashing the bottle on the speaker's head. There was more mimicry of hand-to-hand combat as he drifted out of the kitchen.

He made his way through the rooms. He saw no one he recognized. It was hard to see in the low light, and some people, in the middle of conversations, had their backs to him. He did not want to go around tapping on shoulders or craning his neck conspicuously. He felt self-conscious despite the anonymity afforded by the darkness. He regretted not getting a drink while he was in the kitchen, not only because it had been a while, and because alcohol was helpful in these situations, but because without a drink in hand he felt that much more out of place.

He ended up by the gas fireplace below the mantel and mirror. Solid blue flames licked over fake logs with bulky knots, radiating a dry and passionless heat. No smoke, no ash. Just a steady dull and decorous burn. He stared at it until his eyes began to hurt, letting the competing voices behind him blend into one festive, gibbering blur. When he looked up again, his eyes had hung a scrim of fire between him and the world. He could see only the vaguest shapes, the crudest outlines of people and walls, and then only at his periphery. He waited for the image to dissolve, but before it did completely a familiar voice said, "Well, look who it is."

He blinked to quicken his vision, which helped, but he didn't think it could be possible. "Ben?" he said.

"Lauren and I were just wondering where you could be," Ben said.

"We had plans," he found himself saying, "earlier in the evening."

"Where's Amy?"

"She's home," he said. He added, "Not feeling well."

"Oh, no," Ben said. "The flu?"

"Flulike," he said. "Where's Lauren?"

Ben turned around as if to locate Lauren. When he turned back, he spoke at a much lower register. "Listen, buddy, to your left, at ten o'clock? I'm going to pivot you, okay?" Ben reached out with his beer in hand and turned him a fraction. "Now she's at noon, right over my shoulder. See her? Do you know who that is?"

"She's beautiful."

"Beautiful? Buddy," he said, "do you have any idea who that woman is?"

"I don't know who any of these people are," he said.

Before he could study the woman any closer, he felt a hand on his arm. The grip was thin and hard, shrill, and when he turned to face the gripper, he was face-to-face with Amy's old friend. "Well," he said. "Do you know that we've been looking for you?"

"Stay right where you are, Ben," she said. "I have something important to tell you." She turned from Ben and addressed him. "Walk with me."

With her grip on him now tighter, she led him through the rooms quickly, much faster than he'd meandered through them on his own. "What the hell's going on?" he asked. "We've been looking for you all night, and you're having a goddamn party?"

"You promised to wait for me!" she said to a group of people who turned to her all at once.

"Oh, I won't tell it without you," a man said, and someone laughed.

She turned back with a smile that quickly disappeared.

"Hey," he said. "Are you listening to me?"

"Can you please wait?" she asked, without looking at him.

"Where are we going?"

She returned him to the foyer. She finished what was left in her glass and placed it on the floor.

"Should you really be drinking?" he asked.

"It's cranberry juice," she said. She opened the door, and they stepped out into the hallway. She waited for the door to close behind her.

"Who invited you to this party?" she asked.

"Who invited me?" he said. "No one invited me. We had dinner plans tonight, the four of us, and you stood us up."

"I'm sorry," she said. "We did not have dinner plans."

"I'm afraid, yes, we did," he said. "We made a huge spread for you guys and bought some very expensive meat, and then I come here and find out you're having a big party."

"Now, why would we throw a big party on a night we had plans with you?"

"Why wouldn't we get an invitation if you were throwing a big party?" he asked.

She didn't have an answer. People considered her pretty, but she had puffy cheeks and a pouty mouth that had annoyed him from the beginning, even against his will. He had wanted to like her at first, but her kind of mouth he associated with spoiled brats, and her voice didn't help, nor did the words she spoke. He felt sorry for that baby.

"Can't answer that, can you?" he said.

"Let me ask you something," she said. Her mouth, trembling a little, had never looked more punitive or ugly. "Why do you pretend to like us? Why do you invite us to dinner parties when everyone knows you don't like us, that you've been full of contempt for us from the very beginning?"

He was surprised by the forwardness of the question. He was tempted to argue the point. How could she know for certain who he did and did not like?

Instead, he said, "For Amy." She was silent. "Well, you asked," he said.

"This party is by invitation only," she said, "and we specifically did not invite you."

"So you don't invite me or Amy, your oldest friend Amy, but you invite my friend Ben?"

"We met Ben at one of your dinner parties."

"I know how you met him."

"And he and Lauren have since become friends."

"Who was that woman?" he asked.

"What woman?"

"The woman standing in front of me when I was talking to Ben."

"I must not be making myself very clear," she said.

"Okay, forget it," he said, "forget it. You don't want me here. That's fine. But I came because Amy was worried about you when you didn't show up for dinner. So what am I supposed to say to her when I go home knowing that you couldn't come to our dinner party because you have a big party going on yourself, and that you specifically didn't invite her?"

She stared at him. Her arms were folded and her head was a little cocked, as if they were having a lovers' quarrel, but her face was suddenly calm and expressionless.

"You want to know what I think of you?" she asked.

He was having a hard time reading her face. It was now so blank and flat and calm. He had no idea what she was thinking. It was as if she were a different person.

"I think Amy made a terrible mistake marrying you," she said. "I tried to tell her that, but I couldn't do it the way I should have. Amy and I have nothing, absolutely nothing in common anymore, and I'm sorry but I blame you for that, because it's so awful to have to see you and talk about you, and to think that she's going to be alone with you for the rest of her life just breaks my heart."

He began to walk away. He stopped and turned back. "You're barbarians," he said. "Both of you."

"Don't come here again," she said to him as he was walking away. "Don't call, either. Not tonight, and not tomorrow."

"I can't wait to go home and tell Amy. She's going to love this."

"I wish I could say I cared," she said.

He took a taxi home. In the backseat, he replayed the conversation again and again with such intensity that he began to grit his teeth. He couldn't believe all the many awful things she had said to him. They were outrageous, offensive, and final. He hardly saw anything out the car window, but he could vividly picture her mouth and then the blank expression that had preceded her outburst, which worked him up even more.

When he paid the cab and stepped out, his anger had lessened considerably through too much concentration on it. He wanted it to take hold again with its strangling grip, so he thought of the kitchen: all those dishes in the sink, the expensive meat spoiling on the butcher block.

He walked through the front door and called out to her. He went through the apartment to the bedroom. The bed was unmade in that corner where she had lain reading her book, and the book itself was on the duvet, but she was not there. He glanced in the bathroom before leaving the bedroom and walking back through the apartment, this time turning on all the overhead lights. He stopped at the closet and took an accounting of the coats, then he hurried on to the kitchen, where everything was as it had been a few hours earlier, including her rings on the counter. He was that future self in search of her that he had many times foretold but always dismissed as an impossibility. She had left him. It was dizzying. He had to steady himself against the fridge. He wanted nothing more than to have her there so that he could tell her everything about the evening—what cruel fun, what compensation—but she was gone.

When he returned to the bedroom, she was there. How, he didn't know. She was sitting upright on his side of the bed with her back to him. His relief was immense. He crossed the room and saw in the light coming through the blinds that her eyes were open. She must have known he was there, but she didn't look at him. She just continued to blink in a distant way.

"They were home," he said. He let that sink in. "Can you believe it? They were home that whole time."

She closed her eyes. He prepared what delicious thing he was going to say next. He wanted to go back now and start at the beginning, at the strangeness of those first few party sounds he had picked up on in the hallway. With an economical and unsentimental gesture, she wiped a tear away before resettling her hand on her leg. He wasn't expecting her to cry.

He thought about how worried she had been when they didn't show up. He thought about how much pride she took in her cooking and how much effort she had made for them. It couldn't have been easy, knowing the nature of their good news.

He sat down beside her on the bed and put his arm around her. "They were sleeping," he said. "I had to buzz them so many times just to wake them up. And she was so sorry. She said to me so many times how sorry she was."

She got off the bed and went into the other room. One minute he was holding her, and the next he felt the enormity of the empty bed. He called out to her. She didn't respond. He called out to her a second time. He thought about getting up and going to her, but that was usually no longer helpful. He heard her rummaging through the closet. When she came back in, he was lying down. She switched on the overhead light, which he happened to be staring at. His eyes burned and he turned away. The next thing he knew, she had placed a roller bag on the bed and was unzipping it.

"What are you doing?" he asked.

He couldn't believe what he was seeing. It was a totally predictable thing to do, to pack a bag, and yet completely outrageous. It was both dramatic and futile. Where did she plan to go?

"You're being ridiculous," he said. "Please stop. What does this have to do with me?"

She slowed down. She moved a few more things into the bag, and then, with a gesture that was full of rage and yet halfhearted, she threw in a pair of socks. She seemed to recognize that what she was doing was preposterous, though nothing else appropriate or imaginable had come to her. She stood still in front of the bag. He got off the bed and took her in his arms.

"She just forgot," he said. "That's all. You know her."

She began to sob. She heaved into his shoulder as he held her. Hot tears came through his shirt.

"Why do I have this life?" she asked.

Her arms dropped to her side and she went limp. She cried as if he were not holding her, as if he were not in the room with her, as if he were not in the world at all.

The Valetudinarian

The day after Arty Groys moved to Florida to pursue the leisures of retirement in that paradisal climate, his wife was killed in a head-on collision with a man fleeing the state to escape the discovery of frauds perpetuated for a dozen years under the guise of good citizenship. Arty found himself bereft in a strange land. He knew none of the street names or city centers. His condominium was underfurnished and undecorated. The cemetery where Meredith was buried was too bright and too hot, both on the day of interment and every visit thereafter. Whenever Arty had imagined one of them at the other's funeral, he pictured rain, black-clad figures under black umbrellas, the cumbersome dispersal of the gathered through mud in the lowest of spirits. He saw Meredith leaning down to grasp at one last incorporeal memory as their daughter Gina bent to encourage her to stand, both women weeping—for it was always Arty who had died in Arty's daydreams. But on the day they laid Meredith to rest, golf and tennis were beckoning to retirees in radiant waves of sun, and the fishermen of Tarpon Cove were sporting cheerfully with the devilish snook.

To the surprise of his children, Arty didn't return to Ohio. Over the course of time, they got the sense that their father had stalled, then that his wheels had shifted into reverse, and then that he was heading backward at full speed, toward some oncoming atrocity—their mother's death in reverse, this time entirely psychological. He was without responsibilities after a long professional career, and now he was without the one person, helpmeet and bickering companion, who could shake him out of the recliner and into the world.

His worst instincts claimed him. He started a feud with Mrs. Zegerman, his neighbor in Bequia Cove Towers, a tall condominium building overlooking Naples Bay just south of the Tamiami Trail. Arty suggested in a note slipped under Mrs. Zegerman's door that her Shih Tzu, Cookie, whose incessant yapping came right through the walls, deserved to be shot by Nazis. Mrs. Zegerman accused him of being an anti-Semite; Arty countered that he was not an anti-Semite but an anti–Shih Tzu and that all Shih Tzus should be rounded up. A few days later, Mrs. Zegerman found an unopened box of rat poison near the potted phlox beside her welcome mat, and tensions escalated from there.

In other respects, Arty withdrew. His brooding caused him to lose golf partners and other acquaintances and alienated him somewhat from his one true friend, fit and generous Jimmy Denton. Jimmy had come down to Florida after making a killing in the Danville (Illinois, not Connecticut) real estate market. Jimmy had taken Arty golfing and talked baseball with him, but now it was growing late on Arty's birthday, and he had not yet received a call from Jimmy or from any of his children. He was starting to feel as unloved as he had the day of his ninth birthday, when only two of the eleven guests showed up to his party, a pair of twins who took off their shirts and came together at the arm to show where they had been surgically separated.

He was instantly relieved to hear the first ring of the phone, an old rotary that vibrated with the vigor of the Mechanical Age. He let it rumble and stop, rumble and stop, three full times so that the caller would not suspect how lonely he was. After the third ring he snatched it up. He let the pause grow and then said a very casual hello. It was his daughter, Gina, who lived by herself in a horse stable in Belmont.

"Happy birthday, Daddy!" she cried into his ear. "Happy birthday, happy birthday!"

"Is that you, Gina? God bless you for calling, my girl," said Arty. "Happy birthday to me. Yes, happy birthday to your old man."

"I'm sorry I didn't call earlier, Daddy."

"Oh, I didn't even notice," said Arty.

"We had to put a horse down today. It was very difficult. His name was The Jolly Bones, and he was absolutely everyone's favorite. He was almost sort of human. This one time—"

"My gallbladder's ruined," declared Arty.

"Your gallbladder, Daddy? How did that happen?"

"Yes, my gallbladder. Dr. Klutchmaw says it has to be removed. First a low glucose plasma concentration, then the heart, now the gallbladder. I have never given a thought to the gallbladder my entire life, but evidently it wears down like an old tire. I didn't mean to make such terrible decisions."

"What decisions were those, Daddy?"

"Klutchmaw tells me I could have prevented this if I had stayed away from fatty foods forty years ago, but no one gives you a manual, Gina. No one hands you a manual."

"I wish you wouldn't be so gloomy, Daddy. Not today. Not on your birthday."

"I want you to do yourself a favor and stay away from fatty foods, my girl, because a worn-out gallbladder is no walk in the park. Klutchmaw has a man who plans to remove it, and that means going under the anesthetic, and I may be diabetic. I'm waiting on the test results."

"Well, that sounds good," said Gina. "But what about today, Daddy, what do you plan to do on your birthday?"

"If I had known about any of this forty years ago, I wouldn't be so gloomy today, but no one gives you a manual. The cigarettes ruined my bowels, and I smoked them only ten years before I heeded the warnings. When I go, I have a feeling it will be because of the lungs or the bowels and not the heart after all."

"Do you have a golf game lined up today, Daddy?"

"I'm too fat to play golf anymore," said Arty. "It's a good thing you called when you did, sweetheart. I was just about to go into the kitchen and attack the Oreos."

Gina stayed on the line until she was called away. They were having a little ceremony for The Jolly Bones. She encouraged Arty to get out of the house for what remained of his birthday and to have a good time, maybe by riding his bicycle.

The sun was never so part of the earth's essence as when its golden meniscus quivered at the edge of the horizon just over

Arty's balcony, coloring the clouds and restoring to the sky all the pastoral visions of the earliest era, and filling his condo (furnished with wicker and cushion) with the light of a dying day.

After finishing the Oreos and three glasses of milk, Arty struggled with himself not to dial a number long committed to memory. Doing so went against Klutchmaw's express instructions, and it might tie up the phone right as someone was calling to pass along kind birthday wishes. But in the end he reasoned there was no point aging another year if you couldn't spoil yourself. A familiar voice answered after only half a ring. It was Brad. Brad put in the order for a large meat-lover's pizza and a two-liter Sprite. Anxious about tying up the line, Arty nevertheless announced that it was his birthday.

"Happy birthday, Arty," said Brad. "How old are you?"

"Yes, happy birthday to me. Thank you, Brad. I'm a composite sixty-six, but that doesn't tell the whole story. I've lost much of my aerobic potential and put the lungs at about a hundred. I put the legs at eighty-five. How old are you, Brad? They don't give you a manual, you know. I don't want you to be shocked when they tell you they're coming to pull out all your teeth."

"Arty, man, the other lines are screaming. Can we talk tomorrow?"

"I'll talk to you tomorrow, Brad, you bet. God bless for calling. Happy birthday to me."

"Happy birthday, Arty."

By one of those good fortunes of timing that lonely people long for, the phone began to ring just seconds after Arty set down the receiver. This racket of activity gave the impression of momentary pandemonium and brought joy to Arty's big day. Again, he let the phone ring three interminable times before answering, and then, as the mouthpiece traveled through the air toward his lips, said casually, as if to someone in the room with him, "...think they're going to have a wonderful season this year. Hello?"

"Dad!"

It was his son, Paul, calling from San Francisco. Paul worked in a hospice where he sat among the terminally ill and watched them die. Arty was proud of him—Paul had given his life to a good cause—though not as proud as he would have been if Paul were the owner of a chain of hospices scattered across the country, pulling in profit margins of 30 percent or more.

"Oh, Pauly, God bless you for calling," said Arty. "Happy birthday to me."

"Is there someone there with you, Dad? Should I call back?"

"No, it's just my friend Jimmy Denton. You know Jimmy. We're sitting here talking baseball. You know how I love talking baseball with an old friend."

"Well, I'm just calling to wish you a happy birthday."

"I talked to Dr. Klutchmaw's office today," said Arty. "It doesn't look good."

"Remind me," said Paul. "Which one is Klutchmaw?"

"Dr. Klutchmaw is my internist. He tells me the manufacturer is recalling the stent. There's a flaw in the damn thing. It's not fair, Pauly."

"They don't hand out manuals, do they, Pop."

"No, they don't. You think your heart stent is going to last you forever, and then the manufacturer recalls the damn thing."

"Well, everything's okay here. The children are fine, Dana's fine. Matter of fact, she's sitting next to me and wants to wish you a happy birthday. Here she is."

"Hold on, Paul, hold it just a second before you give the phone to Dana. I want to tell you something, son. Now listen to me, Paul. Odds are, you're going to get fat. You're going to get goddamn fat and you're going to get the gout. You're going to have hypertension and high cholesterol, and you're going to be put on drugs with the worst side effects. They'll make you sweat in odd places. You won't be able to focus or count. Your children will grow distant. Dana will be dead. And you'll be lonely, Paul. I should have told you this years ago, to prepare you, but I didn't know it myself. I just want you to be prepared."

There was a pause before Dana's voice said, "Hello? Is that you, Arty?"

"Oh, hello, Dana."

"Happy birthday, Arty!"

"God bless you. Happy birthday to me."

Arty spoke to his daughter-in-law for a while about heart stents, gallstones, impacted bowels, insulin shots, and stomach ulcers before he announced that he was being referred to an oncologist for twinges that might indicate a tumor.

"Oof!" cried Dana. "Meredith, you can't do that, honey, you're too big! Arty, Meredith just ran into the room and jumped on my lap. I'm on the phone with Grandpa, honey. Do you want to say hi to Grandpa? It's his birthday today. Say happy birthday to Grandpa."

A great battle of wills commenced behind a fortress of muffled static that collapsed totally in brief intervals during which Arty heard Dana scream, "Meredith Ann! Talk to your—!" and

Meredith howl as if in terrible pain, before a silence prevailed and a teary Meredith said, "Hello?"

"Hello, Meredith. It's your grandpa."

"Hello," said Meredith.

"Happy birthday to me."

"Happy birfday."

Like many older people who find themselves on the phone with children of unstable attention spans, Arty began to talk nonstop, flinging at his granddaughter every expression of pride and love, interspersed with questions intended not to sate a genuine curiosity but to confirm Meredith's continued presence on the other end of the line. Arty was convinced that she had no interest in him, that as far as little Meredith was concerned, he was as good as dead. This provoked the panic that fueled the blithering that he hoped might overcome Meredith's annihilating silence. He asked if she knew what an internist was.

"An internist is just a doctor," he explained. "My internist's name is Klutchmaw. I'm not crazy about him, but he takes my insurance. One day you'll understand what an important measure of a good doctor that is. Do you like going to the doctor? I don't like it myself because it always means there might be something terribly wrong with me. You should be very happy that there's nothing wrong with you yet, Meredith. You have your teeth, you can go outside and run around, your bowels have yet to liquefy."

Arty was silent a moment. Where was he going with this conversation, and would her parents approve? Yet he persevered, for when if not now to relay to her the stealth of years, the inexorable betrayals of the body, the perfidiousness of the eventualities?

"They don't give you a manual, Meredith, and who's going to prepare you if not your grandpa? I'm not going to go pussy-footing around your bowel movements on account of your young age, because one day you're going to wake up and wonder why the world perpetuated treacherous lies against such a perfect creature as yourself, and I want you to look back on your old grandpa and remember him as somebody who told you the truth about what's in store for you, and not as one of these propagandists for perpetual youth just because right now your constitutionals happen to be nice and firm. Do you know what a constitutional is, Meredith? I will tell you."

Meredith dropped the phone and ran out of the room. Arty spoke tinnily into the carpet. After a while the phone went dead. A few hours later Paul came upon it on the floor of the bedroom and wondered how he could have left it there, of all places.

Arty had hoped Jimmy would call, but after his conversation with Meredith, despite his importuning eyes, the stolid black machine remained mute. He imagined a conversation with Jimmy, who, knowing that it was his birthday, would indulge him, on this one day only, as he complained once more that neither Bob Sherwood nor Chaz Yalinsky invited him to play golf anymore. They made a great foursome, Jimmy and Arty against Bob and Chaz. But now he had no one to play golf with, no friend but Jimmy, no companion in life—not even one person who might call him on his birthday.

The doorbell rang. Mrs. Zegerman's Shih Tzu pierced the air with high-pitched barks, which ordinarily felt to Arty like an ax whooshing around his head, but as he rose from his recliner and moved from rug to Spanish tile, he tried not to let it get to him, because someone, someone, oh someone was at his door! He dismissed speculation of a late delivery of flowers from one of his children in favor of his old friend Jimmy Denton, there to take him for a beer after shaking free of Jojo, his lusty and calisthenic Oriental wife, who had never liked Arty and made no attempt to hide it. But just as he had taken hold of the doorknob, he realized with a sinking heart that it was probably not flowers and probably not Jimmy Denton, but Dusty, Brad's counterpart, there to deliver the meat-lover's and two-liter.

It was not Dusty.

Standing opposite him, partially lit by the bulb shining from its gaslight cage, was a young woman dressed in a miniskirt of stretch fabric and a bosomy blouse of silver lamé. Beneath her makeup lay a pallor that had been set in place by long, hard winters. Her hair, straining to be blond, had washed out into a color resembling sugarless gum after a long chew. It fell to her shoulders in two coarse and frizzy cascades. She carried nothing in her hands, no purse, no personal possessions of any kind, but when Arty opened the door she raised her hand and dimmed her eye, taking one last drag on her cigarette before dropping it to the tile, where it landed with a tap, and extinguishing it under a bright silver heel.

"You are Arty Growsie?"

"Groys," said Arty.

"Your friend is Jimmy?"

"Jimmy Denton?"

"Is not necessary to know last name."

Arty was pretty sure the woman was a prostitute. He was at his core a fearful, law-abiding, overly cautious man, yet he let

her walk past him without a word. She was spritzed for a cheap
night at a loud club. Before shutting the door he sensed, by
way of Cookie's silence, Mrs. Zegerman at her peephole, holding the trembling dog to her crepe-paper chest.

Arty closed the door. The girl took a seat on the wicker sofa,
and a minute later Arty had situated himself next to her, not
so close as to fall within the weather of her communicable dis-
eases, but not so far as to appear rude. He was touched that
Jimmy Denton would do this for him. The last time he'd seen
Jimmy, at the dog track, Jimmy had said that Arty's yapping
was as annoying as his faggot cousin's at family gatherings.
Arty had been going on about Bob and Chaz just as one of
Jimmy's dogs had come in dead last. Arty excused himself,
bought a hot dog and a jumbo pretzel, which he ate in the car,
and drove home. They hadn't spoken since.

"Well, God bless you for coming," he said to the girl, reaching out to touch her hand but pulling back in time. "God bless
you and God bless Jimmy Denton. It's my birthday, and I was
feeling lonely."

"Ridiculous for handsome and strong man ever to feel
lonely," the girl said.

"I am no longer handsome and I was never very strong,"
Arty said. "I'm fat and I have a bad heart and my internist has
warned me that I'm on the very cusp of diabetes."

The girl said, "Two requirements to continue." She reached
into her bra and pulled out a condom and a blue pill. "Condom
is necessary to use during making love. Erection pill is added
expense but is paid for already by friend of yours."

Arty giggled. "Well, happy birthday to me," he said.
"Happy birthday to old Arty Groys! But, no, I'm afraid I can't

take that pill. It is expressly forbidden by my internist, Dr. Klutchmaw. It interferes with the nitrates I take for my bad heart."

"Do you need pill to make penis work?"

Arty nodded.

"We give it good try, then," the girl said as she stood.

Arty surprised himself by reaching out and grabbing her hand. "Wait," he said. "Don't leave. Have you eaten? I have a pizza coming. We could have dinner."

"You eat greasy pizza when you have bad heart?"

"Please, sit down."

The girl sat.

"Pizza is one of my compensations," Arty said. "I don't have to take a pill to eat a pizza. Well, to lower my cholesterol and blood pressure, but that's different. I eat the pizza and take those pills, but I don't die. I take that pill, I could die. I could have a heart attack."

"Friend of mine from my country swallowed twenty-four pills with liquid pipe cleaner and then took razor blade and cut open left arm from wrist to elbow," said the girl. "Now she lives in North Carolina and works at Holiday Inn."

A stunned abatement of his own concerns stole over Arty and forced him to look at the girl more closely. She stared back at him with the neutral innocence of a child waiting obediently for the start of a piano lesson.

"She survived?"

"Now she is married to American undertaker who steals all her money, but he doesn't beat her, so is good for time being. He fought for America in Vietnam War. Did you fight for America in Vietnam War?"

Her questions ended not in an inquisitorial lilt but with a descending, matter-of-fact thud.

"I was in the service from 1963 to 1966."

"Were you shot?"

"Shot? I was never shot. I fixed chairs and typewriters and other things. I never left Texas."

"I have been shot twice. Here," she said, "and here." She showed him two scars, each a quarter-sized debit of loose yellow skin, one in the stomach and one in the leg.

"What was *that?*" he asked.

She lifted her blouse again. "This? From exploded appendix. Ambulance driver taking his sweet time. Nurse and doctor taking their sweet time. Everyone is taking their sweet time while I am drowning in poison. I am in hospital twenty-six days."

"How old are you?"

"I am eighteen, baby."

"Eighteen?"

"Sorry, I am not telling real age to anyone."

Arty looked at her again. Though he guessed that she was no older than thirty, her pale demeanor and sodden dye job had consigned her to an eternal middle age. He imagined her on her days off lighting cigarettes from noon till dawn, imagined them burning down in rooms defined by drawn shades and muttering talk shows. He saw the crow's-feet that worked against her beauty, but he also saw the beauty. She must have a robust constitution, he thought, immune to colds and despair, unsentimentally surviving. He knew that if he had been born into the same conditions, he wouldn't have made it to ten years old. He had said it a hundred times, a thousand, a hundred thousand, to whoever would listen, but now he merely thought it, with that shock of having discovered that it contained the truth, after all: They don't give you a manual.

"I have question," she said. "Life is so tough, you are afraid of one little pill? It is one little nothing. You take it and we have good time. Maybe I come back next week. Every week we have good time together, and you no longer sit on this nice sofa and think, Oh, poor me, I'm so lonely, I'm such lonely old man."

She drew closer. He was starting to like her overbearing perfume. She placed the pill on his knee. He stared at it. He had never had to consider this option before. He rarely met new people; he was too scared of rejection. Yet here was a girl willing to take him in her arms and kindly ignore the humbling sight of him blundering his way toward ecstasy. And those stern warnings to heart patients not to take such pills—weren't they likely to be, at least in part, the exaggerations of executives afraid of lawsuits?

The girl straightened herself on the sofa and reached around her back and untied something essential. She lifted her blouse to reveal the kind of breasts that Arty believed were seen up close only by men who dealt cocaine and played professional football. There was disbelief, and then there was what passed beyond the realm of the comprehensible into the sensuous world of warrior-kings. Dusty arrived with the pizza. Arty ignored the doorbell.

Mrs. Zegerman resembled a mosquito. She had long thin limbs and a small, very concentrated face whose severe features were drawn dramatically forward, culminating in a sharply pointed nose.

She had passed the day waiting for an apology from Ilsa Brooks, with whom she had had a falling-out after arguing over a movie they had seen together on a recent Sunday afternoon. Ilsa thought the film had been a return to the screwball romantic comedies of the 1930s, but Mrs. Zegerman wanted to know in what 1930s comedy was everything "F this" and "F that." Isla told her to get with the times. Mrs. Zegerman responded by saying that matters of common decency were timeless, and now the two women weren't speaking.

She was preparing for bed when she thought she heard the doorbell ring again, and again her first thought was that it was Ilsa, come to apologize. It would be such a relief to have her matinee partner back again, but as her bare feet left the Persian rug for the red Spanish tile, she remembered that Ilsa had returned north to Chillicothe on Wednesday, and she quickly reverted to the opinion that her former friend's ideas of both movies and morals were wanting.

Through the peephole, she watched the pizza boy pointlessly ringing Arty's doorbell until she could take it no more. She stepped out into the open-air vestibule to explain the situation: Arty Groys was inside that condo with a woman who had appeared half-naked on his doorstep. Mrs. Zegerman was convinced that the two of them were in there interrelating. It was shameful and disgusting. It was also interfering with commerce.

"Arty's in there with a woman?" the boy said. "Our Arty?"

She had no idea what he meant by "our."

"You sure he didn't just kick off?"

"He's not dead," she replied.

"Well, goddamn," the boy, a Newport smoker and native of

Florida, said. He removed the pizza from its space-suit pouch and placed it with the Sprite to one side of Arty's door before nodding goodbye and galloping down the stairs. "Tell him it's on the house!" he cried.

This was not the first time she had watched that boy go. He was such a well-tanned boy. Perhaps he surfed. For a brief second, she felt her body warmed by the sun and her head pillowed by the sand, while out in the distance, doggie paddling on his board, Dusty waved to her between surging whitecaps.

She stepped back inside her apartment and picked up Cookie. She decided to wait there for Arty to emerge with his floozy so that she could give him a piece of her mind. A moment later, Arty's door slammed shut like a shot. Mrs. Zegerman jumped to the peephole in time to catch a glimpse of the departing girl, who fled down the same stairs as her delivery boy while quickly tying her blouse, carrying her silver heels in one hand. Mrs. Zegerman naturally assumed she had been repulsed by the sight of Arty's horrible penis. Then a long time passed at the peephole, and Arty didn't come out for his pizza.

Mrs. Zegerman found Arty on the floor of his living room. She was thrown into a panic at the sight of him that emptied her mind entirely of common sense. She simply did not know what to do, and the sensation of helplessness resounded with the one thing she remembered in all her years: the terror of the day that Mr. Zegerman had stumbled while walking along the wharf and hit his head on that utterly purposeless green metal thingy. She remembered the seep of his warm blood through her summer dress as she cried out for help. Now it was her neighbor whom she might have loved for years and years, so swiftly and completely had she been struck dumb by his perfect helplessness. He had collapsed between wicker sofa and coffee table, his legs hairless and white as wax, his stomach a great pale mound, and his face as pinched and pink as crab shell.

"Oh, thank God," Arty said when he caught sight of his neighbor. "Call the paramedics, Mrs. Zeger—"

He was cut off by a terrible grip, a twisting vine-strangle of the heart—but his words had the intended effect. Mrs. Zegerman kicked into high gear. She rushed over to him throbbing with adrenaline and restored him to respectability by returning to its rightful place the underwear that had been dangling around one ankle. Then she clamped his left arm like a nutcracker over her slender neck and supported his bulk all the way to the elevator. She planned to get him downstairs and to drive him to the hospital in her Mazda. If she had learned one thing from the death of Mr. Zegerman, it was never to put your faith in the promptness of men who drive ambulances. But they had to wait too long, much too long, for the infernal elevator, which liked to clamor down below with buckling metal and other echoes of motion the minute the call button was pressed, dallying there for untold minutes before zooming right past, up and up, to some grander view of Bequia Tower. At last she told Arty that they would have to take the stairs, and she carried him over to their brink and started the descent with her weighty dying charge. On the final flight, however, they got tangled up and he went flying, bouncing down brutally step after step, while it was everything she could do to catch the banister and not follow after. She took one look at the twitching body that lay in a yellow pool of security light and, scared that she had killed him, raced upstairs again to call an ambulance.

The first two days, he was incommunicado, lost beneath a breathing apparatus when he was not in surgery. To move out of the I.C.U. into a regular unit took him another five days, by which time she had found his insurance card and called his children.

"What does this mean?" Paul asked.

"Will he live?" Gina asked.

"How will he get around?"

"Who will take care of him?"

Mrs. Zegerman assured them that she would take care of Arty. Not only did the children not object, they seemed to imply that there was simply no one besides Mrs. Zegerman whom they would have looking after their father at this difficult time.

"He's always spoken so highly of you," said Paul, who had heard Arty speak about Mrs. Zegerman only when denigrating her dog. "And we, for one, the children, I mean, are just so grateful knowing you're there."

Arty's knee was in terrible shape from the fall. Once his heart had fully recovered from what proved to be a mild heart attack, he would need to have an operation to determine the extent of the ligament damage, followed by a long regime of physical therapy. His weight posed a significant impediment to a swift recovery. The orthopedic surgeon predicted that it might be as long as a year before her husband walked again. Mrs. Zegerman had succeeded in convincing everyone that she and Arty were engaged to be married and did not correct the surgeon's error.

*   *   *

Mrs. Zegerman walked the corridor to Arty's room. The coarse, almost particulate sun showering in through the window there filled the small, antiseptic space with a false radiance. There was no need for it, as his children's flowers had wilted and died days earlier. Now the competition between the outside heat and the meager central air made the room feel claustrophobic and unpleasant. These things might have gone unnoticed had her first observation not covered her in a thin sweat of panic: the bed was empty. Arty was not in his room. Had he had another heart attack? Had he died overnight? Gone! Overnight! She wished she had never gotten involved. Oh, dammit. The dog was enough.

Suddenly the toilet roared and the bathroom door was thrown open. Arty Groys came staggering out, favoring his good leg while fiddling with the fly of the pressed trousers she had brought for him the day before. Mrs. Zegerman was beside herself, for he was walking in defiance of the doctor's predictions. She rushed over to him with exclamations of dismay.

"What are you doing up and about, Mr. Groys? Your knee is in no condition to be walking around, to say nothing of your heart."

"God bless you, Mrs. Zegerman, God bless you," he said. "But the heart has never been better, and the knee is only knocked off center a little. If I had remembered to take that cane with me, I would hardly have noticed a thing."

Mrs. Zegerman saw an ivory-handled cane in the far corner of the room. She turned to Arty with surprise, as though she had just found something unsavory in his sock drawer. She had been with him practically every waking hour since he entered the hospital. Where had that cane come from?

"We must get out of here, Mrs. Zegerman," Arty said. "We must get over to Jimmy Denton's house."

"Who's Jimmy Denton?"

"Jimmy Denton is the man responsible for all this, God bless him. He never visited or sent flowers, but no doubt his Asiatic wife is to blame for that. She must have closely guarded from old Jimmy the fact that I was dying only ten miles away. She has always been jealous of our friendship. Now, it's better we do this on the sly. Are you ready?"

"But you haven't been released yet, Mr. Groys."

"Mrs. Zegerman, I must see Jimmy Denton. He knows how to put me in contact with the girl who saved my life."

Mrs. Zegerman had been under the impression that she had been the one who'd saved Arty's life. "And who is that?" she asked.

"No time for particulars, Mrs. Zegerman," he said. "Now take a peek and tell us if the coast is clear."

And so Mrs. Zegerman suddenly found herself sneaking Arty Groys out of the hospital. They simply walked down the corridor, into the elevator, and out the main exit. Arty did remarkably well with the assistance of his cane.

"They did a wonderful job in there," he said, "but I'm happy to be leaving. Too many people die in hospitals. You'd be safer on a Chinese beach with those scavengers and their rusted circuit boards. And would you look at that," he added when they had crossed the threshold and entered the day. "The sun is shining so gloriously. Before that heart attack of mine, I would have just called that glare."

Jimmy and Jojo Denton lived in a gated community whose thriving heart was a golf course dotted with sun-dappled ponds—a perfectly manicured oasis of hurricane-proof Spanish colonials, manatee mailboxes, and geriatric promiscuity. Mrs. Zegerman, staying put at Arty's insistence, watched her hobbling neighbor get out of the car in front of a gaudy palazzo and limp across the dense lawn. He returned not five minutes later, hastily shutting the door.

"Jojo dropped a dime, Mrs. Zegerman," he said. "She's always been a meddlesome woman. We have to get to East Naples, and pronto. Apparently they all crowd into a single apartment unit. The thought of it just tears the heart out of my chest."

"Who are you talking about, Mr. Groys?"

"The young lady who saved my life."

"I have news for you, Mr. Groys. I am the one who—"

"Mrs. Zegerman, I beg you. Jojo Denton had sicced the police on someone very dear to me. There's no time to lose. Please put the car in motion and head east."

Mrs. Zegerman thought it was imperative to get Arty Groys home, to set him up, with his bad leg and weak heart, in bed or on the recliner, with pillows and remotes and restorative liquids, and to discuss his dietary preferences so that she would know what to buy at the grocery store. She was looking forward to a long convalescence. The obvious indifference with which the widower's children treated their father's caretaking guaranteed that she would preside with crowned authority over many months of incremental improvement.

But Arty's sudden mobility had made her heart sink. The long months of sequestered progress vanished instantly, casting doubts on her hopes and dreams, and his oblique agenda in East Naples reduced her to feeling like a mere chauffeur. They were heading down a swath of highway raised out of the wet-lands, past a schizophrenic landscape of saw-grass prairies and strip malls, where the road signs warned of panthers and the billboards advertised outdoor malls and alligator zoos. Mrs. Zegerman came to understand, through Arty's roundabout explanation, that his friend Jimmy had spent two hundred dollars on a birthday present for him. There had been no way for Jimmy to blame that extravagance on his time at the dog track, so to protect that beloved pastime, he had had to come clean to Jojo that very morning. His wife immediately put in a call to the Collier County Task Force Initiative, with whom she had worked in the past to enforce speed limits in her subdivision and to establish random sobriety tests at crucial intersections. At some point, after putting two and two together, Mrs. Zegerman stopped listening.

Arty guided them into an apartment complex and through a maze of speed bumps. To the right and left stood building after gray generic building. They went past a dumpster center and a large barricade of metal mailboxes while Arty searched, squint-eyed, for the right apartment. They had to circle around three times before he found it.

She braked quickly at his command. He turned away from the apartment complex to look at her. "Thank you for the ride, Mrs. Zegerman," he said. "There's no sense in mixing you up any further in all this. I'll take a taxi home."

As he climbed out of the car, she was speechless. She was hurt, she was confused, and, most of all, she was angry at herself for feeling an absurd but overwhelming sensation of abandonment.

"Mr. Groys," she said, "don't you need your cane?"

"No, thank you, Mrs. Zegerman. That cane just slows me down."

"But you shouldn't even be walking!" she cried.

"Isn't it something?"

He slammed the door. She immediately flung herself over the seat and manually rolled down the window. "Arty!"

He turned with surprising grace and peered back at her from a distance of a dozen feet. "Yes?"

She was propping herself up on an elbow, craning her neck and staring at him through the open window like an alien creature. He stared back at her in the full dazzle of the sun. "Arty," she repeated. "In all the years we've been neighbors, why have you never asked me my first name?"

Arty stood awhile in silence before limping back to Mrs. Zegerman's Mazda and bending down to the window. "I don't know," he said. "What is it?"

"It's Ruth," she said. "Although my friends call me Ruthie."

"May I call you Ruthie?"

She had straightened out and taken hold of the steering wheel again. She turned to stare out the windshield while he peered in at her. She replied without looking over. "I suppose that would be fine," she said at last.

He did not know what to expect and imagined he might encounter some specimen of pimp—the dagger-dark madam or tracksuited thug—but it was a petite black girl who answered his knock and asked him who his appointment was with. After Arty had described her (he didn't even know her name!), the black girl led him to a dental-office love seat in a gloomy room whose only distinctive feature was a mounted poster of a Budweiser logo, and disappeared down the hall of what was otherwise the kind of apartment that recent post-grads pile into as one pursues acting, the other a law degree, a third some kind of entrepreneurial scheme, and a fourth the dollar tips handed out at gentlemen's clubs. The barren despondency of the place depressed him and challenged his resolution, arrived at in the earliest hours of his recovery, to see the girl again. He had been living as a dead man for years, and without her sudden presence in his suffocating cloister, coaxing and tempting him, he would certainly have died a dead man. He planned to offer to retire any debts she might have accrued and to furnish her with education funds. Was this preposterous? Would she laugh in his face?

Something prompted him to rise and walk to the window. He widened a gap in the cheap venetian blinds and squinted out into the sun. He had a view of the entire parking lot, and he saw, once his eyes had fully adjusted, Mrs. Zegerman's tiny sedan parked beside a gleaming black motorcycle. What was Mrs. Zegerman still doing there? He narrowed his squint and focused all his attention. She was crying. She had rested her chin against the top arc of the steering wheel, and the tears were falling down her troubled face. He had never seen her cry before. It was possible that until then, he had never really seen her at all. After a moment she righted herself, retrieved a tissue from the glove box, and blew her nose.

His attention was called away from Mrs. Zegerman by first one and then a second squad car pulling up outside the building, their sun-muted siren lights twirling unnoticed by anyone but him. His still-delicate heart came to a stop, as if suddenly cast in stone, only to shatter into pieces when it came charging back. Jojo Denton had remarkable pull. Four Collier County police officers stepped out and began to confer, then approach, by which time he had let the blinds snap back and was rushing toward the rear rooms.

He found her brushing her hair in front of a bathroom mirror. She turned and saw him standing in the doorway. She backed up at the mere sight of him—his eyes were still bruised from his fall, his forehead was pinkly scarred, and his pale, sweaty demeanor was ghastly. She issued something quick and terrified in a language he could not identify. "I don't believe it!" she finally cried in English. "I leave you one hundred percent dead man."

"You remember!" he said, happily but a little breathlessly. "I have survived and I have come to thank you, but first we have to get out of here. Jojo Denton dropped a dime, and the cops are right outside."

"Cops?"

"Is there a back exit?" he asked.

He didn't wait for an answer. He reached in and grabbed her hand and pulled her with him. He limped briskly to a sliding glass door in one of the bedrooms, where he struggled to undo the stubborn metal lock. While this was going on, he turned to her and said, "Do you remember the pill?"

"The pill?"

"The one I refused to take," he said. "You persuaded me to take it, do you remember? How did you know I needed to take it? How did you know just what to say to me?"

"You stupid!" she cried, having taken over. "Glass door is open whole time!"

They left just as a thundering knock landed on the front

door and reverberated through the apartment. He raced ahead of her, his knee be damned, and turned back to speak as they descended the back stairs. "How did you know?"

"Know what?"

"How did you know what to say to get me to take that pill?"

"Are you so stupid? I am prostitute!"

"No, no, it was something more," he said. When they reached the bottom of the stairs, he brought her to a halt and said, "I want to take care of you. I want to pay your debts. Let me pay your debts and fund a college education for you."

"This is very tired routine," she said, "and not good timing."

Upstairs, invisible, they heard the commotion of the ensuing bust. They hurried across an expanse of treeless yard to the front of the apartment complex. Cars washed by on the street. He refused to allow his knee to bother him as he ran beside the girl. He was happy that he had survived to declare his intentions. He had no ulterior motive. What she did with his offer was up to her.

Soon they were several blocks away. There was no cop or squad car in sight, and he could have stopped. But he didn't stop, not even when he saw Mrs. Zegerman. She turned away from the road to gape at him as she slowly drove alongside him. She rolled down the window and shouted something he couldn't hear on account of his heavy breathing. He smiled at her. He let go of the girl's hand and waved. He wanted to tell her many things, like how sorry he was to have been cruel to her dog, and how surprised even he was at how well his leg was holding up. Or maybe his strength was only an illusion, just as it had been one summer when he was a boy playing baseball, that day he attempted to steal second and was forced to slide as the ball neared the infielder's glove. The infielder missed, and the ball shot past, and when he saw he was free for a run to third he jumped up and took off, despite the hairline fracture that would make itself known (through the pain that came with a dawning awareness of all that lay in store for him) only later, long after he had passed the third-base coach, gesturing like mad, and made it home, graceful as a dancer, bodiless, ageless, immortal, a boy on a summer's day with a heart as big as the sun, with all his troubles, his sorrows, his losses, still ahead of him, still unknown, unable on that still-golden field to cast any of their tall, unvanquishable, ever-dimming shadows.

The Pilot

Leonard hadn't heard from Kate Lotvelt in two weeks. Not that he absolutely should've necessarily. He and Kate, they weren't ... were they friends? Well, yeah, they were friends. They were acquaintances. They'd met twice, once at the producer Sydney Gleekman's yearly blowout, and then, a few months later, at the actor's dinner party.

Kate's invitation had come by email. She was considerate, or she was canny, not to include the addresses of the other invitees. She'd sent the message to her husband and bcc'd everyone else.

From: Kate Lotvelt
To: Eaton Aiken
Subject: Death Is a Wrap! Come for the drinks & stay for the pool.

He'd RSVP'd, but not immediately. Two days after the message came in. Two days plus maybe an hour. And said something like,

Just can't wait. Heading to tax-friendly Winston-Salem in a few days to shoot this godawful underarm commercial. Remember that particular station of the cross? Maybe not, probably scrubbed it from memory. But, hell, work's work. That pilot I told you about is coming along, I think. Gleekman's enthusiastic, or at least Pleble claims enthusiasm on his behalf. But the sad reality is always reality television. It's why I so admire *Death*. It's a sick little fuck-you every week to the swapped wives and tarantula eaters.

Reading this back to himself ten minutes later, Leonard would think, *God,* I do go on and on.

Congratulations, by the way. Three seasons! Goddamn if that's not impressive in this climate. But the show...well, do you ever tire of hearing how good it is? And I thought life was over after *The Wire*. Listen, no need to reply to this long-winded email. You're wrapping! But can't wait to see you at the party. Consider this an RSVP. No way I'd miss it. Not a chance in the world. Hooray! Cheers cheers, Lx.

He didn't expect a reply. It was a mass email—she couldn't reply to everyone who replied. She was busy, she was wrapping the third season of her show. He would have liked a reply. After a few days went by, he'd have liked a reply a lot. Was his email too effusive? Was it a mistake to use the word "sick" to describe her show? Or maybe she was just busy shooting the season finale. Yeah, she was just busy shooting the season finale. Why hadn't he just written back something quick-like? "Thanks for the invitation, Kate. See you then." Then she might have quick-like hit Reply, with a confirmation, and he'd have it confirmed that she knew he had confirmed. Did she even know she had invited him? Sometimes, with email, some programs, you hit All Contacts or whatever, and suddenly you're inviting people you never meant to invite. Of course she'd meant to invite him. He just didn't have any confirmation. That was kind of unnerving. But think about it. Would he then have to confirm her confirmation? That wasn't really feasible. It was just . . . Everything was fine. She was just wrapping. He shouldn't have been so effusive. "Sick little fuck-you": that might have been — no, it was fine — just a little insulting? No, no, it was fine, who knows, not him.

At the actor's dinner party, the night they'd exchanged email addresses, he and Kate had been seated together. Ten minutes passed before his heart would settle. Then they talked about the Guild and its troubles. When he thought she had warmed to him, he peppered her with questions about her show — how she ran a room, what her writing habits were. He tossed hints of his awe but scrupulously avoided rhapsodizing. When, in the past, he had rhapsodized, even to mere cameramen, his first impulse upon returning home had always been to beat the fanboy in him into a permanent coma. After dessert, while the other guests were drinking an expensive port — he'd been dry now sixteen months — Eaton Aiken, to everyone's delight, took off his shoes and, standing on newspaper, painted a mural on the actor's dining-room wall with some old house paint and a stiff brush.

In the days following the invitation, he thought about how different his anticipation of the party would be if he were Eaton Aiken. If he were Eaton, it would be *his* party. He wouldn't

have to worry about anything but what he already had: a 1920s
Mediterranean with a porte cochere, at the top of Griffith Park;
an infinity pool laid with Moroccan tile (he had seen pictures in
People magazine, against his will, waiting in line to buy gum);
money for the booze and the hired hands to serve it; a solo show
at the Getty before the age of forty; and, for a life partner, Kate
Lotvelt. Eaton Aiken hadn't just finished shooting a deodorant
commercial in tax-friendly Winston-Salem.

The night of the party arrived, and still Kate had not sent
her invitees an email reminder. That was usually part of the
protocol: a message saying, "In case you forgot, looking forward to seeing you," etc. It prompted him to ask: was the
party still on? He couldn't be totally 100 percent sure, not
without a reminder, and here it was already the middle of the
afternoon. He was in his darkened room—irrepressible L.A.
sunlight battering the closed blinds, unwashed bedsheets reek-
ing of tobacco smoke—watching DVR'd TV backlogged since
W.-S. and checking-rechecking his email for a reminder email.
Of course the party was still on. If you were Kate Lotvelt,
would you worry about guests coming, or about proper email
protocol? Kate Lotvelt had succeeded beyond the pedestrian
sorrows of social anxiety. It was an awesome thing to behold,
on her behalf, his inbox with no reminder email in it. For others, like Leonard, it was mighty unsettling. Wasn't it possible
that now that she had wrapped, she'd taken better care to select
from her contacts the people she really wanted at the party and
sent the reminder email only to them?

Finally he got a reply from Pleble.

Yo bro, how'd the shoot go? I'm in Indio. Do not fucking go to fucking Coachella. Time was there were a hundred great bands and ten people in the know. Now it's a refugee camp for neohippie fuckheads. What exactly are you asking about a reminder email from Kate Lotvelt? She needs to drop that Romanian douche and sign with me. Back on Monday if you need to talk. In the meantime, why not finish that pilot? Your humble Pleeb.

No help at all. He'd hoped to hear that Pleble was going to the party so that they could go together. Or if they didn't go together, at least he'd know that he'd know someone there. But maybe Pleble hadn't been invited. But if he, Leonard, had been invited, Pleble would have been invited. Kate and Eaton knew Pleble better than they knew him. Didn't they? Now he was thinking that there really must have been a contacts mishap. It would have been nice if Pleble had confirmed or denied that he'd been invited. But Pleble was shrewd. If he hadn't been invited, he wouldn't say, "Kate's having a party? Why wasn't I invited?" He'd say just what he'd said. So maybe Pleble was invited, but he was in Indio, which sucked, because it would have been nice to go with someone, or at least know he'd know someone there. Or maybe Pleble wasn't invited, in which case there must have been a contacts mishap and he shouldn't have been invited, either. Either way, now things were even more uncertain than before Pleble's totally unhelpful and possibly calculating email. Maybe he wasn't even in Indio! He was tempted to write Gleekman and ask him if he'd been invited and if he was going or at least if he'd gotten a reminder email. But he didn't want to give Gleekman the impression that he was feeling insecure about his place at Kate's party. That would send the wrong signal. The pilot was but a polish away.

Kate Lotvelt was the creator of and showrunner for *Death in the Family,* as well as its head writer and a member of its star cast. The show's meandering, almost nonexistent plotlines revolved around the Bonfouey family: Connor and Jean, adult son Mike and his wife Sally, teenage daughter Irene, adopted Korean child Koko, dog Revolution, and neighbors the Wilkes-Barres. In every episode, someone died. Connor murdered Jean, or Jean set fire to Sally, or Mike was wrongfully executed, Irene caught a cold, Koko fell into the pool, Revolution was shot, or the Wilkes-Barres were poisoned by Sally's green-bean casserole. Everything taboo and unpleasant about death was lampooned: disease, hospitals, the squeamish austerity of burn wards, funeral homes, unbearable sadness. And by the next episode, everyone was alive again! Everyone was just swell! No memory of last week's suffering and no suspicion of the coming doom. The question for the folks at home was: Who will get it this time? And how? The best episodes left him breathless. There was the effectiveness of its satire, but also the stupefying entertainment of its metaphysics. How, week after week, did Kate Lotvelt turn something so gruesome and frightening into the funniest show on television?

He hoped to do the same thing with *Life of the Party,* but it needed a polish. It needed a fresh set of eyes. Somebody smart. A pair of eyes like Kate Lotvelt's. But might it be better, rather than going to Kate's party, to stay home and polish the pilot so that on Monday he could give it to Pleble, who could give it to Gleekman, so that they could all finally start seriously engaging one another? And if he stayed in to polish the pilot, he could stop worrying about whether he'd been invited to Kate's party or if he'd know anyone there or why he hadn't received a reminder email.

But half of this business was networking. And what was the better option—going to the party of the year, to which he'd been invited, and networking with actors and executives? Or returning home to Atlanta to die? Those, it felt to Leonard, were his choices. So what the protocol for air-kissing hello kept shifting on him? So what he'd never established an easy routine with beautiful people? So what that when he got home from parties like this one, finally removing his sunglasses for the night, he did nothing but play back, soberly and obsessively, all his many insufficiencies? Should he have been more casual? Intense? Fawning? Detached? Happy? Was happy an option?

He needed a new pair of eyes on his pilot. Someone smart, like Kate Lotvelt. He also needed a new pair of sunglasses. For as long as he could remember, he'd taken refuge behind a pair that had belonged, originally and iconically, to the Suburban Gangster from New Jersey. Actually, more specifically, to the Suburban Gangster's loser cousin. The would-be-actor cousin who gets it in the show's last season—his sunglasses. They had disguised Leonard's drunkenness and, later, dimmed the unbearable glare of the sober world. But then he left those sunglasses behind at the CountryAir Motel in W.-S. and hadn't been able to locate a replacement pair, the gangster show having concluded seasons ago, and fashion having moved on.

He was debating inviting his roommate. On the one hand, he'd have someone to go with. On the other hand, his roommate was a musician, and he trembled before the mystical competition of a musician's nightlife. What if he invited him and he said no? His roommate had something going on nearly every night, always more vibrant and exclusive-sounding than the pale thing he generally had going on, and so he felt it better to withhold the invitation than risk suffering the indignity of rejection, even if that rejection was due to a simple conflict of interest, like preexisting plans, for example. It was hard not to take even preexisting plans personally. Because what if, for instance, his roommate secretly delighted in having preexisting plans because of how little he cared to entertain Leonard's lesser invitation, even when tonight that "lesser" invitation was a party at Kate Lotvelt's? If, that is, that invitation still stood. Which he couldn't be 100 percent sure of. If the invitation did not stand, the last thing he wanted was to show up at Kate's with his roommate in tow and discover that Kate didn't remember meeting him at Gleekman's or at the actor's dinner party and had no idea why he'd come and brought his roommate—who, no doubt, would have preferred doing something in the subterranean world of musicians. So he decided not to invite him.

He did, however, ask to borrow his jacket.

He didn't like to borrow other people's clothes, but there was something about that particular jacket that would make arriving at Kate's party less intimidating. What was it? He wasn't sure where he got the idea that it was the jacket of a perfect badass, because it wasn't like he paid a lot of attention to fashion. Maybe he'd seen it on someone. He'd definitely seen it on his musician roommate once, and that guy was totally cool. If he had to show up to Kate Lotvelt's without his sunglasses, which made social situations easier and served his sobriety like a crutch, but which he'd lost a week earlier in W.-S., at least he'd have on that cool motherfucker of a jacket.

His roommate was on the sofa, curled over his guitar, shirt-less, wearing white rayon gym shorts and a pair of cowboy boots. Above him on the wall hung a buck's head wreathed with leis and party beads, a steel helmet from the Second World War hooked on the tip of an antler. When he stopped strumming to make notations on the sheet music fanned across the coffee table, Leonard put his head out of the kitchen and said, "Hey, so what do you have going on tonight, Jack?"

He was still unsure—maybe he should invite him. If he, Leonard, wasn't invited, it would be comforting, despite what-ever embarrassment, to have Jack beside him, someone even less invited than he was. And if it turned out he was invited, it would be nice to have Jack there to eliminate any awkward walking alone through rooms.

"Giving myself an ultimatum," was Jack's reply as he leaned back on the sofa. "Write three new songs by the end of the day or shoot myself in the head."

Leonard was not infrequently put to shame by Jack's work ethic. He watched Jack lean forward again, pick up his little pencil, and make another series of quick notations. His example made Leonard conclude that the only thing to do now was to stay in and put a polish on the pilot. Was there really any other op-tion? What was he thinking, going to a party, even a party like Kate Lotvelt's, when the pilot, with a little work, could be given to Pleble, and he could maybe say goodbye to tax-friendly back-waters and start taking real meetings with real people at all the big studios around town? So that was settled. Stay in, work on the pilot. Finish the pilot or shoot himself in the head.

"Why, what's going on with you?"

"Oh, there's this party," he said, drifting over with his coffee to a lawn chair that served the two roommates as a living-room recliner, "but I don't know. I think I'm going to stay in and work on the pilot. Do you have any interest in going to a party tonight?"

"How's the pilot coming?"

"It's close. I'd say real close. Which is why I should stay in. But I don't know. I was going to ask if I could borrow that jacket of yours, in case I go. Would you like to go?"

"Hey, man, I'm not joking. If I don't write three new songs tonight, look for me in the woods with a bullet in my brain. Fucking L.A.—it's worse than Nashville! Don't worry, I won't do it in the house. What jacket?"

He described the jacket, and Jack got off the sofa and returned from his room with it. And it fit! He asked Jack how he thought it fit.

"Fits perfect," said Jack. "You want it? It's yours."

"You don't want it?"

"I never wear it."

"Why not?"

"Not since what's-his-name started wearing it, and then everyone else started wearing one just like it."

"Since who started wearing it?"

"You know, what's-his-name. The real-time antiterrorist cop dude. What's his name?"

"Oh," he said as it dawned on him—the cop, the jacket, the show. "Right," he said. "I know what show you mean. He wears a jacket like this one?"

"Don't get me wrong," he said. "It's a great jacket."

Leonard returned to his bedroom, removed the jacket, and

set it on the bed. Goddamn it! It fit, too. He was determined not to go to the party now, certainly not in that jacket. Show up at Kate Lotvelt's dressed like the real-time antiterrorist cop dude? He might as well go dressed as the Fonz! No way. He sat down at his desk. He was going to stay in and put a polish on the pilot. He called up the document on his computer. Finish the pilot or die. Finish it . . . or live forever in backwaters promoting morning-fresh roll-on with no unattractive residue.

He was inside the car and debating with himself when his mother called. It was curious timing, and he considered not answering it. The ritual of her call was now so invariably a part of the day that it had moved beyond its initial phase of support and nurture into something self-conscious, liturgical, and annoying. She'd been calling every day for sixteen months—by now their little exchange was entirely formal and meaningless. But was it meaningless *this* time, right as he was sitting in the parking lot of a bar, debating? The day was almost over in Atlanta. Usually she didn't wait this long. Wasn't that a sign? He would have preferred to let her go to voicemail, but tonight he wasn't so sure. It might be wise to pick up tonight. Maybe she'd say the thing that would get him out of that parking lot and headed in the right direction.

So he did, he picked up, and after they bantered about nothing for a few minutes, she said, to no one's surprise, "Will you do me a favor today, Leonard?"

He abided by answering, "What's that, Mom?"

The unvarying reply was, "Will you please not take a drink today?"

"I won't take a drink today."

"Will you promise me?"

"I promise you, Mom."

"Thank you," she said.

"Okay. Thanks for calling, Mom."

"I love you, Leonard," she said.

"I love you, too, Mom."

"I'll talk to you tomorrow," she said.

She tried. She did all she could. But it just wasn't enough, and he got out of the car and went into the bar, where he sat down before all the familiar labels of his misery.

He stared, and soon his small and laser-focused eyes began to water. The labels lost all crispness, and the glass bottles dissolved into rays of heavenly light. The bartender broke his trance by tossing a coaster Frisbee-style down to the grainy bar. "What can I get you?" he asked. Leonard paused theatrically, as if debating, then ordered the whiskey and chaser he came in for. The whiskey and chaser was all he needed to make it to Kate Lotvelt's party unconcerned about his place there and at ease without sunglasses or jacket, and sufficiently fortified that, should the opportunity arise, he could ask Kate to have a look at his pilot. It was only twenty-four pages. It was only a whiskey and chaser.

He turned away from his fellow patrons as he waited for his drinks to arrive. Better not to engage, or even be looked at, while falling off the wagon. Was that what he was doing? After sixteen months of sobriety, he was just gonna...fall off? You betcha he was. His brain was killing him. He needed something to help him turn it off, especially if he was going to find the courage to talk to Kate. So he angled away from his fellow patrons in private shame and found himself staring into a separate room.

It was a dining room of some sort, decommissioned and

darkly lit, with red vinyl booths and a cash-out station with an old silver register. Next to the register sat a bowl of peppermints and a toothpick dispenser. By some intuition—something having to do with all the television he'd watched that day—he was drawn off his bar stool and over to those toothpicks. He removed one and studied it. He placed it in his mouth and let it roll around, releasing its mildly minty, mostly wooden flavor. Then he removed it and stabbed the air with it sharply, screwing up his eyes and mouthing a few words, as if chastening someone. The gesture was filled with righteous instruction. Then he put the toothpick back in his mouth and stood there, staring hard into the imagined eyes of the recently chastened. He moved the toothpick around, still staring, transformed.

Who did that?

That was the Coach. The Coach did that.

The Coach was on every Friday night, winning games, teaching his boys how to be men.

He took the toothpick from his mouth and stood there. It was curious. First his mother's call, now this.

He turned in time to catch the bartender setting his drinks down. He went back to the bar and paid for them, telling the man he had been called away. He left a courteous tip. On his way out, he removed a number of toothpicks and put them in his pocket.

Now we detour away from Leonard's mind, he thought, and enter a new realm. A realm of high spirit, few words, and the best of intentions. To want to be the Coach—there was no better intention than that, for any man. That was what that toothpick could do for him. It could locate within him what he shared of the Coach's character. A character limited, yes, by the emotional restraint of athletic-minded men, their incurious and circumscribed intellects, but also one liberated by an expansive, uplifting, and victorious heart. The noble Coach was always victorious, even in defeat.

He stopped at a sporting goods store to purchase a blue windbreaker to go with the toothpick, and to go with the blue windbreaker a matching hat whose stiff bill he worked hard to break in on the drive over to Kate's.

Was it weird to be impersonating the Coach? Leonard had never been the coach of anything. He was borrowing character from a TV character, a scripted, writer-engineered fiction—was that, uh...maybe a little pathetic? No, it wasn't pathetic. The Coach was a great man. He had focus, and backbone, and an admirable lack of ceremony. He wasn't trying to impress. He was just trying to win tomorrow's game. Even his circumscribed intellect was enviable. People thought drink was the enemy. It wasn't drink. The enemy was thought—looping destructive gnawing thought. Drink was just a cure. A cure, in the end, worse than the disease. Wasn't channeling a good man better than destroying yourself with drink? Yes, it was. No doubt it was. Also pretty fucking sad and pathetic? Stop it now, enough thinking. He was pulling into Kate Lotvelt's house. He got out and let the door hang open as a one-armed valet came forward. Distracted by the sounds of the party, he drifted away without his ticket and a few seconds later was startled when the valet chased him down.

The 1920s Mediterranean was resplendent in the night breeze. Party lights climbed the pink columns of the porte cochere. He walked past a baroque fountain tinkling vigorously before the bougainvillea as distant laughter mingled with a d.j.'s midtempo beat. The party was evidently under way. Feeling left out, he slowed, wondering: Had he gotten the times wrong? Or had they changed the times? Perhaps in that follow-up email he had never received? He turned to beat a retreat back to his car and home when one of Kate's *Death* co-stars (a silver fox in a Scottish kilt) came around the corner with his long-gowned companion and forced Leonard to swivel back in the original direction, and together—or, rather, the one party pushing the other along like a snowplow—they went around the side of the house to the pool and terraced garden. At their feet lay a glittering view of downtown. The diving board rattled like a tuning fork, and a second later a cannonballer came up cackling in the white wake.

Breathing shallowly in the hostile embrace of a hundred strangers, Leonard remembered the Coach at the last minute. Remembered that he no longer needed to impress these folk. He was there to mingle, to booster, and to nod tight little hellos at everyone, touching his fingertips to his toothpick. When he saw an opportunity, with clear eyes and a full heart, he would go up to Kate Lotvelt and ask a favor of her. He had the pages of his pilot carefully folded lengthwise in his back pocket.

He entered the house. All the chic and beautiful guests were paired off or tripled up or twined together in intimate laughter. He knew none of them. He tried to look casual as he drifted past: sufficiently out of place, as the Coach would have been, but never so lost and hopeless as to undercut his core dignity by fleeing the room. Eventually he took an open seat on the nearest sofa. To his left sat a delicate blond back whose animated shoulder blades mocked a passionate conversation. He turned in the other direction and found two more backs and four shoulder blades. He chewed his toothpick nervously until he worried that anyone paying the least attention would take him for a lone shooter, and he left to find a bathroom. Ten minutes later, having read all the labels on the medicine vials, he flushed and departed. He searched the enormous house for the kitchen and something nonalcoholic to drink. When at last he found it, the catering people seemed so put out by his request that he retreated empty-handed. He watched from some doorway as two men in rich red shadow played a game of pool. At last he drifted back to the room that led out to the patio, and there he spotted Kate.

Wow, was she tall. He'd forgotten that about her, just how tall she was. He went straight up to her—well, to those gathered around her, as she was just then regaling a little circle of rapt admirers with an anecdote about hangers. He couldn't follow along because he'd missed the beginning and was nervous.

"So this is the guy I go to now to buy hangers," she said. "Travis at the Hollywood Split—my hanger guy."

Someone asked her how many hangers she'd bought.

"Twenty hangers, four bucks."

"Wait...*four?* Didn't you owe him five?"

"He's a homeless guy selling hangers on the highway," she said, "and you're not going to haggle?"

Everyone laughed.

"Hey, I need some hangers," someone said. "Which highway?"

"Excuse me," he said. "Kate?"

She turned to look. Everyone else did, too. He brought his hand up to his toothpick and nodded at the man on his right. Then he looked back at Kate and nodded at her, too. "You got a minute?" he asked her, his voice quivering most un-Coach-like. He had removed the toothpick from his mouth and was pointing the soggy end at her. It had turned to mash between his teeth and now looked stringy and gross, almost obscene. He quickly crumbled it up in his hand.

"Sure," she said. She turned and gently touched the arm of the person directly to her right. "Excuse me a second," she said.

He took the opportunity to pocket the old toothpick and replace it with a fresh one, which he twitched back and forth in his mouth. "I'm awful sorry to take you away like that," he said. He'd grown up in Atlanta, which wasn't Texas, where the Coach lived, but it was the South, so the thick accent he was suddenly deploying wasn't totally disingenuous.

"Is everything okay?" she asked, as if he might be with cater-ing, bringing to her attention a snafu with the hors d'oeuvres.

No, she had no memory of him from Gleekman's or the dinner party, didn't recognize him, hadn't invited him, couldn't explain why he was there now. "Uh . . . ," he said, "Sorry, I . . . uh . . ."

Then, with relief and amazement, he watched her puzzled expression iron out and that grand smile familiar from TV beam his way. "Wait a minute—is that Leonard?" she cried. She reached out and pulled his cap off. "It is you! What are you doing under that cap, Leonard?"

"Yeah, I'm wearing a cap," he said.

"You look like what's-his-name," she said. "You know, the Coach."

"The Coach?"

"From TV. You watch that show, don't you? You have to, if you don't already. It's a great, great show. Anyway," she said. "What's your favor, stranger?"

"Did you invite me?" he asked.

"What?"

"Did you invite me here tonight?"

"Of course," she said. "What do you mean? You're here, aren't you?"

"I just wondered if you meant to."

"Of course I meant to," she said.

"I thought it could have been a contacts mishap."

"What is that? What is a contacts mishap?"

"You know, like when you press Select All and don't mean to."

"I've never heard of that," she said. "Hey, it's nice to see you. How's your pilot coming along?"

"My pilot?" he said. He was surprised to be asked. "My pilot's close, I think. It's real close."

"That's great," she said. "Congratulations."

"I think it just needs a polish," he said.

"That's fantastic."

"Hey, and congratulations to you."

"Thank you," she said.

"On wrapping the third season."

"Thanks. Yeah, thank God. It's nice to be done."

They talked about wrapping the third season, and then she was called away. She didn't leave without touching him on the arm and promising she'd be right back. He felt enormous relief. He walked straight to the bar and ordered a whiskey. While it was being poured he asked himself what he was doing and told himself to shut up. He had the second one in hand before he had finished the first.

After that he moved freely from room to room and from

group to group. He double air-kissed and sometimes only single air-kissed the beautiful people, one of whom, inadvertently, he felt he stabbed in the cheek with his toothpick a little on his way in. But he fled that little clique and on the whole found the party to be a relaxed and easy affair. Disappointment in himself nagged at him, but he ignored it. He went up to Eaton Aiken and spoke his name while staring at his back. Eaton was forced to pivot away from the conversation he was in. He was wearing a maroon velvet suit coat and a pair of strikingly red slip-on sneakers. "Yes?" he said.

Leonard extended his hand. "Leonard," he said. The Coach's Southern accent was giving way to something more English-y. "We met at Neil Connell's dinner party."

"Neil who?"

"Connell. He's an actor. Bloody good actor, too. He plays— well, he did play, until they canceled the show, now he's just..."

"Connell," Eaton said. "Name's vaguely familiar. Vapid little fuck? Self-satisfied?"

"Who? Neil?" he said. "I don't know. Maybe."

"It was an empty night we all spent together. You never removed your sunglasses. Somehow you remained sober. Are you an alcoholic? No, you have a drink. I was a recovering alcoholic once. Before I became the alcoholic I am today." He rattled his glass. "This feels more like home, you know. Cheers."

"Cheers," he said.

"You can't toast with just ice. It's bad luck."

"I was just on my way to the—"

"You sat next to my wife. You looked at her all night as if she were Helen of Troy. I painted that cocksucker's wall with house paint and raised the resale value by a hundred thousand dollars, for which I got paid back in blather. Is that the night you have in mind?"

"I think maybe."

"Right," Eaton said. "And how have you been?"

"Okay," he said.

Eaton excused himself to get another drink.

Leonard spent more time on the sofa, then returned to the bathroom where he tried to steady himself in the mirror, then he was on the patio doing shots. Toward the end of the evening, he followed the producer Sydney Gleekman down the hall and caught him coming out of the bathroom. Gleekman was told, without his soliciting the information, that the pilot was close, the polish was only a pilot away, and that he should expect a draft from Pleble on Monday.

"Remind me again," asked Sydney. "Who's Pleble?"

"Mark Pleble? My agent? We met you at your big party last year?"

"Does he work for CAA?"

"No."

"William Morris?"

"No."

"UTA?"

"He works for a kind of boutique agency, I guess."

"Oh, sure," said Sydney. "I know just who you mean. Have him send it to me. Ah, there she is. Excuse me."

Sydney left, and Leonard headed back to the bar. Was the party winding down? He thought it was; there were fewer people around. He knew he should probably go home but chose instead to have a final drink with a guy who was maybe famous.

Then he went outside and lay down in a chaise on the far side of the pool.

He took the pilot out of his back pocket and started to read by the watery blue light. He lit a cigarette. He wasn't sure he was in the right frame of mind to properly evaluate what he had written, but as he read, and smoked, and read, and smoked, something new occurred to him. His pilot was a comedy in which the main character was a recovering alcoholic who, every episode, found himself surrounded by drunks. Every episode— or so he envisioned it; there weren't any "episodes" yet—his character had to work hard not to drink. He was the "life of the party." The title was ironic; the life and humor came from the many drunks all around him. But could that conceit be sustained for an entire season? What if, he thought, just what if his character got on and off the wagon from episode to episode? Then the question became (every Thursday on CBS, ideally), will he or will he not take a drink? Just like *Death in the Family*. But instead of, "Who will die this time?" people will ask about his show, "How will he fall off the wagon?"

He fell asleep. The embers of his cigarette caught the pages of his pilot, which began to smolder and burn. He coughed and woke himself up, looked down and found his new windbreaker on fire. He tossed the burning papers aside and leapt out of the chaise. He tried patting the flames down, but they wouldn't disperse; they seemed only to spread. He wasn't sure where the fire started and where it stopped. He *was* the fire. He threw himself into the pool.

He came up to the surface. He was coughing now not from the smoke but from having taken in water. Where was everybody? Was that dawn breaking in the sky so high up? The water was slippery. He couldn't get purchase. Every once in a while, the Coach, too, had too much to drink, and you could see in his eyes just how much he regretted it. He tried to call out for help, but his voice was muted by another intake of water. Sobering infusion of chlorine. Desperate silent eye-popping wheezing. Reach for the closest edge! Which way? He spun, grew dizzy, took in more water. How quickly the new dawn was disappearing! Shimmeringly at first. He was going under, losing the surface to the depths. Happening? He hit bottom. Well, what better position from which to launch himself back into life? Only the water had turned impossibly heavy all around him. His body shuddered violently. And yet his eyes were open and everything was suddenly so clear. Of course Kate Lotvelt's party was on, had always been on, with or without a reminder email. Why did he trouble himself over such trivial matters? He doubted his worth on so many levels and so frequently missed the point entirely. That was no way to live!

This was just like the pilot. Not *his* pilot, of course. Kate's pilot. *His* pilot was still a polish away. But he'd cracked it! Before falling asleep he knew the way forward! Or had that been a dream? At the bottom of the pool, his arms continued to make little arcs of almost peaceful effort. Here, at last, the pith and core of a deeper understanding came into focus. There was no need for RSVP anxieties. No need for fraudulent costumes. Time to get serious! He'd stay in tomorrow and finish the pilot. He was never going to take another drink again tomorrow. First thing tomorrow, he was going to put aside his hang-ups and retire his shame, and when he wrote to Kate Lotvelt to ask her to read his pilot, he would also mention without fear of being a fanboy how in love he was with her very true show.

A Night Out

Tom and Sophie waited twenty minutes in a ripe sauna for a transfer at West Fourth Street. When at last the train rolled into the station, they boarded a car full of infernal heat. They went through the doors to the next car over, but it, too, lacked air-conditioning. The whole train did. There was a rancid smell. They returned to the first car. It seemed cooler there, somehow. But there was no escape.

Slogging out of the subway, they passed a fat woman on the stairs, begging help from anyone willing. Tom absentmindedly rubbed the downy dollar bill folded in fourths between his fingertips. A found thing: He had been worrying it since they left Cobble Hill.

"That one's not well," he said, eager to change subjects as they reached the street. "What was that on her face, a staph infection?"

"Who was that woman?" Sophie asked.

"The homeless woman?"

"No," she said.

"Oh, you mean Clara," Tom said. "Just now? Clara."

"Who is Clara?"

"Clara? I've told you about her," he said. "The analyst? Who they weren't going to fire, but then they did?"

Sophie made no reply. Tom, out of the corner of his eye, glanced at his wife who, head down, arms folded, walked at a slant as if into a winter wind. She was chilled. They were passing over a steaming subway grate, the panting crosstown bus shedding exhaust at curbside—and yet there was Sophie, chilled to the bone. Tom sighed. "Look," he said a minute later. But she was no longer beside him.

He turned. "Sophie?"

She was ten feet away, at a dead stop on the sidewalk. He thought at first she was staring at him, boring into him. But no, her eyes weren't looking at anything, really. She was in her own world.

"Sophie," he said.

And that was when she turned and walked away.

"Sophie!"

What the hell? He stood there, uncomprehending, hot, annoyed: a man abruptly in the middle of something. She walked past the subway entrance, turned at the street corner and disappeared.

It would be the lost minute, the hesitation that would cost him. When finally he started after her, turning at the corner where she had turned, he caught only a glimpse of her—white thighs, black boots—just as she was turning again. How had she gained ground so quickly? At the next corner, an absence of streetlights conspired with an abundance of trees to cast shadows everywhere. He squeezed past the cars packed tight at the

curb and crossed over while calling out her name. Halfway
down the block, he quickened his pace. He reached the corner
in a run just as a taxi was pulling out, sweat pricking at him.
He looked both ways. He looked behind him. She was gone.

She watched from the top of the stoop as he ran past, then
doubled back the way she came until she reached the bright
entrance to the subway.

Aside from a seated woman with a stroller, the northbound
platform was empty. A busker's song grew louder as she went
down the stairs to the southbound. Here no train had come
for a while, and all the riders, sunk in a torpor with drawn
faces, were thickly assembled. But she couldn't miss Clara,
the analyst: knife-blade thin with jet-black hair, she pulled a
paperback book from her leopard-print handbag. Sophie had
spotted her just at the moment a shirtless man had had enough
and yanked a final leg from his sweatpants. "Too hot!" he cried
out, balling up the pants and throwing them down. "Wouldn't
happen in France!" Sophie slipped past him while everyone else
stared. He wedged his feet inside his high-tops and, naked now
but for his boxers, resumed a shuffle down the platform.

As Clara, the analyst, turned from the man and began to read
her book, Sophie drew up behind her.

She didn't know how she knew. She just knew. Tom wanted
not to have seen her, then he shifted with a smile and a loud,
"Clara!" Clara was surprised to see him, or acted so. Tom introduced his wife. Clara complimented Sophie's handbag. Their
little conference inconvenienced those trying to pass on the
stairs, so they soon said goodbye. Clara continued down to the
subway, and Tom and Sophie joined the crowd on the street. In

the silence that followed, Sophie realized that this, too, was another thing she would have to endure and then assimilate into their reconciliation.

The train pulled in. Those waiting to get on bottlenecked at the open doors, teased by the cold air, as the departing passengers stepped off. Clara was among the first to board. Sophie followed her with her eyes until she disappeared inside the car, then she strained for a final glimpse through the inadequate window. But for what? Greater understanding? Proof of her continuing right to come unhinged?

They were having dinner with her parents. Stupid to have run away. They would be late now. All the same, just as the doors were closing, Sophie got on.

Tom muttered to himself. He threw up his hands. For a moment he seemed determined in his stride, only to stop, turn, and stand, arms akimbo, before drifting back the way he'd come. He removed a tissue from his pocket — machine dried, like the dollar bill, and now soft and stiff — which collapsed completely at the first wipe across his brow. Tossing it into the bin at the corner and missing, he tried her cell phone again, but she wasn't picking up.

He returned to the subway. He used the last swipe on his card to go through the turnstile, glanced down the northbound platform (steadily filling up now) before taking the stairs to the southbound. He arrived just as the taillights of a departing train flashed red in the dark tunnel.

They rattled along at top speed.

The three boys with the boom box circled one another before

the center doors, full of a nervous energy. "Ladies and gentlemen," said the handsome one, dark and lean in his overlong wifebeater, "ladies and gentlemen, we apologize for the interruption." The other two whooped and clapped to whip up a wearied crowd that was also a captive audience. Their clapping fell into a rhythm when the music started, and the first boy dropped to the floor to break-dance. When the shorty took center stage, he made a flying leap onto the support bar and hung there with so little effort, he might have remained horizontal all the way to Far Rockaway.

Sophie stared past them. Clara, the analyst, was sitting beside a man who, having dragged a floor lamp onto the train with him, was holding it steady with a fist. The pull switch swung around and around as the car shuddered along the tracks.

Okay, so she was prettier. That was settled. What else?

On the subway again after that long struggle just to get to the Upper West Side—that was never part of the plan. What was next? Ordinarily Sophie was unsurprising, an Oberlin and a Harvard Medical School grad in her first year at Lenox Hill. An emergency-room doctor frequently on call who, when not on call or at the hospital, was with Tom, her husband. Familiar, predictable, dependable Sophie.

The show ended with the shorty going around the car for tips. The train pulled into the station and the boys got off. A man boarded with a mountain bike, steadying himself on the support bar with his fingertips while holding his bike by the seat. The front tire appeared to leer at the standing lamp until, in tandem with the handlebars, it turned away in an attitude of contempt. By the time the train pulled out again, Sophie had taken a seat next to Clara.

She really was pretty, wasn't she? Even in profile. Cute little button nose, nice skin, dark, swanlike neck. She looked special. What should Sophie do now that she could do anything? Maybe nothing. Or maybe she should ask Clara a question. But what? Nothing too complicated. For instance: "Do you feel special?"

Some errands a man runs without taking much notice of the world around him. The weather, or what's outside the cab window. What's outside the window is life, rioting life, but the man experiences only his own blind impatience to get past it all and on to the errand at hand. A man is a monster. He turns away from the crowds, the buildings, the bridges, as if this alone will speed things up, urging the cabbie on in all sorts of ways.

That was how Tom traveled whenever he paid a visit to Melissa.

Melissa was an aspiring actress (waiting tables to pay the bills) who lived just over the bridge, in Queens. From Tom's office in Midtown, it was a twenty-minute ride to Melissa's one-bedroom, depending on traffic, during which time he failed to see a thing. In retrospect, it was like traveling by portal. One minute he was in his office on the eighteenth floor, then *whoosh*... he was on rumpled bedsheets taking Melissa from behind. Huddled with colleagues in the lobby of a law firm... *whoosh*... fucking Melissa on the sink of a dive bar in the East Village. Walking through Central Park with Melissa before she had to start her shift... *whoosh*... back on the bed he shared with Sophie, calling out hello when she came through the door.

Something a man cares about even less than what's out the window when he's traveling by portal: the feelings of others.

Now Tom *was* what was outside the window, as taxi after taxi passed him by on Columbus. He was no longer traveling by portal; he was going around in a circle. A circle of hell, in this heat.

Still, he noticed as little as he did in the portal, only now it wasn't pleasure he was after. It was an old perception of himself. Tom wasn't just some animal on the street. It was never his right to go around fucking whomever he wanted to fuck. He was a married man. His marriage vows had bound him to his wife and to the world of decent men. There were just some things decent men did not do.

"Hey, it's me," he said into his cell, planting a foot on top of a fire hydrant at the same instant a fire truck blew past. "Look, it's not her. The woman you're thinking of wasn't a colleague. She worked for a caterer. Call me."

She hadn't wanted any of the details when he came clean, and he obliged.

He thought it would end in one of two ways. She'd hate him and leave. Or she'd forgive him and stay. He never imagined it would somehow be both.

Tom ended the call, looked off, and ran the cuff of his shirt-sleeve over his sweaty brow. The guy on the bucket outside the bodega was looking at him. Tom sensed it and went back to worrying the dollar bill in his pocket.

"Could be you," the man said.

There was no mistaking who the man was addressing. "Pardon?" said Tom.

"Could be you," the man repeated. Then he pointed.

Behind Tom, on the the window of the bus-stop shelter, was

an ad for the current Powerball. The jackpot was up to $347 million. Could be Tom. Why not?

"Sure," Tom said. "Could be any of us."

"Not me," said the man. "Never been lucky."

When the company he worked for had announced the first round of layoffs, they'd let go of one analyst out of every five. That had seemed enough to make a second round unlikely, but a few months later they'd let go of the same percentage, only now from a smaller pool. His colleague Clara had been part of that round. Tom had held on until the fifth. He'd always been lucky.

He looked down the street both ways once more, then walked up to the corner and peered in all four directions. The hot white lights of the taxis came at him unevenly, as if the streets were wilting. He gave up and went inside a bar.

He put his elbows down and gestured to the bartender. The stale smell of old beer, the stadium array of bottles and the booths sunk in darkness in back had had the effect of reminding him of illicit afternoons with Melissa. He did not want to be reminded. He wanted to be out of the portal and headed to dinner with Sophie, meeting Sophie's parents in a pleasant little place on the Upper West Side. When the bartender came forward, Tom ordered a beer and then asked the name and address of the bar. There was a time when the very last thing he would have done when entering a place like this one was text the details to his wife.

The bartender set the drink down delicately and whisked away the damp money. She made change with one hand while pouring seltzer with the other.

A single room on the small side, the bar was intimate, with

crowded red walls dimly lit by votive candles. It had the effect of a boudoir. Above the bar sat suspended a distressed mirror raked at an angle. Glancing up at it, Sophie could make out most of what was going on behind her. A man at the far left kept moving in and out of the frame, depending on whether he was talking (sitting back) or listening (leaning forward). In the opposite corner, at a small, round table for two, Clara sat alone before a golden glass of wine, her back to the plate-glass window and the Brooklyn street. Sophie had to lean to the left to see more than her hand on the stem of the wineglass.

The bartender came back with Sophie's change and set it down on the bar, but not before soaking up all that dampness with a disintegrating white rag.

So this was it. Alone in the dark, drink in hand, waiting for a stranger. She could see the allure.

Now he was calling, texting. So attentive.

Another round of brief and frantic texts came in. She could delete the voicemails. but the texts were harder to ignore. She slipped off the bar stool and stepped outside.

Hello, Tom

S! where are you? What happened? Did you get my vm?

Where are u

In a bar. Can you meet me or ill come to you

What did you order?

Just a beer but don't have to drink it just tell me where you are

In a bar with a beer. Well, she thought. Not *that* attentive.

*   *   *

Tom's phone went dark; Sophie had popped up out of hiding and just as quickly disappeared again. Nevertheless, he sat glued to the bar for the next twenty minutes, trying to engage her, cajole her, coax her back into an exchange so that he might have some idea how this nightmare would end. The in-laws were waiting.

The volume on the anthem overhead grew noticeably louder midsong. The door opened and another party came in. The bartender was joined by a bar back, and a waitress began going around with a cork tray, taking orders for shots. She asked Tom if he needed anything. "No, thank you," he said. She smiled politely as she turned away. "Actually," he said. "Shot of Jameson, please. Put it on my tab." She went away, and Tom stood up. The seats along the bar, once so plentiful, had nearly filled up now, and Tom felt himself to be in a different bar altogether than the one he had entered. He leaned his stool against the bar as a way to protect his seat—he was debating whether to pay up and resume his search or wait around with another beer—and went outside into the terrible city heat once more, to search in vain for Sophie. The feeling of dislocation continued when he noticed that the front of the bar—really, the whole building before which he stood—was covered in scaffolding he didn't remember seeing on the way in. He had to look hard for the name of the bar, as Sophie would if she ever arrived, and when at last he found it, obscured behind some orange netting, it was not the name the bartender had given him and that he in turn had texted to Sophie. On his way in again, he was held up by at least a dozen people entering at the start of a bachelorette party.

He took up his seat but found himself pressed in on both sides. He shot down his Jameson and resolved to get out of there. He got the bartender's attention, but instead of asking for his tab, he questioned him about the name of the bar. Shrugging nonchalantly, the bartender offered the correct name this time. Tom asked to settle up.

The bartender returned with his credit card, saying it had been declined.

"Declined? No, it can't be," he said, yet he was already reaching for another card.

That one came back declined, too, and when he searched his billfold, he found he had no cash.

In the past, when Sophie discovered that someone she knew was having an affair, she expressed a sincere shock. Then Tom had his affair, and, perhaps to justify his behavior, he didn't just grovel; he pressed on her news of the countless others having affairs, the colleagues and acquaintances, and the friends they shared in common. She began paying closer attention. At the hospital, nurses were having flings with doctors, EMTs with orderlies, and administrators with pharmaceutical reps. Old high school friends back home were divorcing at a clip on account of these same shenanigans. How naive she had been. Within a few weeks, Tom's affair had convinced her that behind the decorum of everyday life, everyone was fucking everyone else. The whole world was conducting one continuous orgy, and the only one fool enough to play by the rules was Sophie.

She had wanted to play by the rules. Hadn't she? The rules kept things safe and orderly.

She watched through the window as her husband's mistress stood and shook hands with the man she was there to meet, perhaps, eventually, to fuck. What had Sophie—innocent, predictable Sophie—been missing out on all this time? What was it like to fuck a stranger? She wondered. She was not herself. She did not ordinarily act vindictively, as she had over the last ten minutes as she stood outside the bar where Clara had led her, canceling their shared credit cards. Tom was without any means of his own anymore, and now he was cut off; she had separated herself from him at last. She should have done it a month ago. Who was Tom when his wife disappeared and his money dried up and his lover was meeting another man in a bar?

Not her problem. She went back inside and ordered another martini.

Tom's father-in-law left his wife sitting alone at a table for four, walked six blocks to a crowded bar on Columbus, and paid to release his son-in-law from the strange bind he was in. Sid was a big man with a small fortune, ill disposed toward the unforeseen, who never appreciated having to leave behind his cocktail. Tom had been trying to win his favor from the first day he met him.

As the two men walked down Columbus together, Tom expected questions that never came. "Thanks again, Sid," he said as they approached the man sitting on the bucket outside the bodega.

"There he is, Mr. Lucky Strike!"

Tom nodded as they walked past.

"Could be you, Lucky!"

"Is that man talking to you?" Sid asked.

"We had an exchange earlier," Tom said.

"Do you owe him money, too?"

At the restaurant, Tom had hoped to find his wife sitting with her mother, but Emily was alone. She looked stranded amid the Friday-night crowd, sipping her Manhattan, surrounded by plates of uneaten appetizers.

"I had to order something, Sid. They wouldn't stop giving me the evil eye. Where is Sophie?"

Emily turned from Sid to Tom and back again. Sid placed his napkin on his lap and drank down the entirety of his glass of ice water. He was still chewing an ice cube, his chin glistening, when he turned to Tom and said, "You want to give us some idea now just what the hell is going on?"

"There's been a miscommunication," Tom said, "that's all."

"What about?"

Both Sid and Emily stared at him, demanding answers. Where was their daughter?

He could come clean, as he had eventually done with Sophie. But a father like Sid? He'd be a lot less forgiving than his daughter ever was. And Sid was a softy compared to his wife.

Their searching looks grew more urgent. The pressure was on. Where had she gone? What had he done?

"Sid, Emily," he said. "This is just a little disagreement between Soph and me. It's unfortunate that it had to happen right before meeting you guys for dinner, but you can't time these things. It will get worked out. In the meantime," he said, "I'm going to ask you both, please, to butt out."

He perspired more hotly in the immediate aftermath of this—he had never stood up to his in-laws before—than he had out on the street, and he took up his water glass. As he drank, he scrutinized Sid and Emily for their reaction. They regarded each other silently, searching for a unified front.

Sid sat back in his chair. "You're right, Tom," he said. "It's none of our business."

"I agree," Emily said. "As long as she's okay. Is she okay, Tom?"

Tom set his glass down. "Thank you," he said to his father-in-law. "And, yes, she's fine, Emily. She's just angry at me, that's all."

His mother-in-law nodded and looked down at her drink. Tom was relieved. A little surprised, too. Oddly... touched. Was he family to these two people? He would not have said so. But now it seemed maybe he was. Seemed they respected him. Treated him as an equal, as one does with family. Who would have guessed that? Not him. No, they could never know.

"Okay, look. If you must know," he said, "we had an argument about how much time she spends at the hospital. I think she spends way too much time there."

"Oh, I agree," Emily said. "She's absolutely killing herself there, Tom. I hope she listens to you."

"Well, we'll see."

"Gentlemen, we should eat these appetizers before they get any colder."

Sid finished his martini. "I want another one of these," he said. "Where's that waitress?"

Tom looked down at his phone. Still nothing from Sophie. All his exhortations had failed to move her. He decided to try something different. "Now you're acting like a child," he wrote from the semi-privacy of his lap. "Your parents are worried sick. We're sitting here like idiots. Can you give it a break for an hour and join us?"

That should do it, he thought, hitting Send. He sighed deeply as he rejoined the company of his in-laws. But he didn't have much time to savor his relief when he locked eyes with Melissa. She had been hailed and was standing between his mother-in-law and his father-in-law in a blue apron and a man's tie, her fine ginger hair up in a bun.

"May I have another one of these?" Sid asked her.

"Well, look who it is," she said.

He had never asked her where she worked when not lending the caterer a hand.

"How are you, Dylan?"

Nor had he given her his real name.

"Are these your parents?" she asked.

All the blood drained from his face. "Yes," he replied faintly.

"We're his wife's parents," Emily said. "Do you two know each other?"

"Your wife's parents," Melissa said to Tom.

"Did you just call him Dylan?" Sid asked.

"Uh, can we have a word?" he said, removing his napkin from his lap. Panicked, stupefied, he failed to rise any further.

Melissa smiled at him viciously. "Yes," she said finally to Emily, turning to her, "we do know each other. Dylan and I were seeing each other until about a month ago, when I just never heard from him again."

"What does she mean, Tom, 'seeing each other'?" Sid asked.

Emily turned to him, her hand over her mouth.

"I don't know," Tom said. "Nothing."

"You son of a bitch," Melissa said.

"Sid, Emily," Tom said, "we're going."

He began to stand when a firm hand took hold of his shoulder. He froze and peered over at Sid. They were eyeball to eyeball, it seemed.

"Sit," Sid said.

Tom sat back in his chair.

Sid stood up. "Get your purse," he said to Emily.

"Did you want another martini, Dylan's father-in-law?" Melissa asked.

"We're leaving," he said.

The man was a stranger. Never had she been inclined to pick up a stranger in a bar. Perhaps she didn't think herself pretty enough. She lacked courage, feared rejection. The truth was, she had only had a total of two lovers in her life. Her husband had had two lovers in the past month.

She stood up, walked over to his table and sat down across from him with her drink. He returned her smile but also looked a little bemused. What was this perfect stranger doing before him suddenly? His companion would be back any minute.

"Who is that?" Sophie asked him.

The man across from her, confused, or amused, or both, said, "Who?"

"The woman in the ladies' room. The woman you've been talking to for the last half hour."

"Uh...a friend."

"A good friend?"

"Uh...well, no, not really," the man said. "More like a friend of a friend. Who are you?"

She said her name was Melanie. She extended her hand across the table, and the man took it.

"Are you going home with her?"

"Excuse me?"

"Clara," Sophie said. "Are you going to take her home?"

"Do you know her?" the man asked.

He looked around as if he might be the butt of a joke, a man suddenly in the middle of something.

"She's prettier than me," Sophie said. "But I'm a sure bet."

"A sure bet?"

She told him that she was going to step outside, where she would be waiting for him. He could take his time saying goodbye to Clara. Then he was free to take her home and do whatever he wanted to her.

"I'm married," the man said.

"So am I," she said.

He looked at her.

"So I take you...somewhere...and then...what?"

"And then," she said, "whatever you want."

"What do you mean, whatever I want?"

"You do to me whatever you want," she said.

He no longer looked amused.

Melissa brought Tom the check for the drinks and hors d'oeuvres his in-laws had ordered, but Tom had no way to pay it. He had no choice but to talk to the manager, who listened to his plight with a stony indifference. He asked Tom to wait, so Tom stood near the front door, getting in the way of every new party that entered. When he wasn't in the way, he was gazing into the dining room, watching Melissa buttonhole another server and point at him until it seemed everyone in the restaurant knew what was going on with the guy up front.

He could leave his cell phone behind, along with his license. When he came back with what he owed the restaurant, he could have them back. That was the best the manager could do. That, or call the authorities and let them sort it out. It was up to Tom.

He was halfway down the block when he heard his name called out. Melissa had his license in her hand and waved to him with it. "Nice to finally meet you, Thomas!"

He turned on Eighty-Second to get away from her. He waded east through a current of heat, in the direction of the subway. He wanted a cab, but he had no money. Sophie had the keys; how would he get into the apartment? He couldn't call her; the restaurant had taken his phone. And he no longer had a driver's license to prove he lived there.

"Hey, look who it is! Mr. Could Be You!"

He didn't reply. He worried the dollar bill in his pocket as he walked past.

Night turned to brightest day as he descended the stairs to the subway. The homeless woman with the staph infection was still on the landing. His Metro card had insufficient funds.

He retreated to the machine where new cards were issued and value could be added to old cards. The display screen informed him that he was a dollar and five cents short. The night's many frustrations caught up with him all at once. "Motherfucker!" he cried, and hit the screen hard with his palm. The station agent looked over. He took a deep breath. Then he remembered the dollar bill in his pocket. Incredible luck! He ironed it out and inserted it into the machine. But of course he was still five cents shy. "A fucking nickel," he said. He swiveled around to find a few people drifting alone through the station. "Anybody got a nickel?" he asked them. No one answered. "Hey, man—you got a nickel so I can get home?" The man ignored him. What a fucking asshole. What was a nickel to him? "Nobody here has a fucking nickel?" he said. It made him self-conscious, and he stopped asking. But he continued to mutter. "A fucking motherfucking nickel," he said as he started to scan the station floor for coins.

Sophie watched as the man took leave of Clara. A married man, meeting a woman in a bar, leaving with a second woman because she had thrown herself at him. Was everyone so depraved, or had Sophie just gotten lucky?

Clara was prettier, but she was a sure bet. There was more power in a sure bet. Sophie had never known.

He came out, and they set off together down Court Street.

"What did you tell her?"

"I rescheduled," he said. "I'll email her later. Doesn't matter. She's just someone looking for a job."

They turned off Court and walked toward the tracks. At the dead end in the distance, the concrete wall was heavily tagged with graffiti; behind it, the subway descended into the tunnel.

Was he attractive, this man she was about to...? She hadn't noticed. She looked over, but the streetlight behind them was faint, and there wasn't another up ahead. The weak moonlight was strongest here. He was...fine. Heavyset. Not her type. Whatever. Didn't matter. They reached the dead end.

"Where are you taking me?" she asked.

"I have nowhere to take you."

"Then where are we going?"

He didn't answer.

What was the name she had given him? Melanie? Melinda? She wondered if he remembered.

"Hey, what's my name?" she asked him.

He stopped and looked up and down the street. In one direction, it led back to the neighborhood's many restaurants and bars; in the other, to an empty lot where the pavement gave way to weeds and the fence curled up along the top like a sardine can. "In there," he said.

"Where?"

He pointed. "Behind that."

She peered into the no-man's-land. There was an earth mover sitting in the sparse grass among half a dozen cars parked at odd angles. It was strange, hostile. Nothing at all as a girl imagines it. But it was closer to the secret way of the world . . . or so she told herself as she reached for the man's hand and took the first step.

The Breeze

She was in the brig when her husband came home. Below her, neighbors reclined on their stoops, laughing and relieved, shaking off winter with loud cries and sudden starts. Someone unseen scraped a broom across a courtyard, the rhythmic sound of brownstones in spring.

"In the brig!" Sarah called out and, with her wineglass at a tilt, peeked down again on the neighborhood. They called their six feet of concrete balcony overlooking the street the brig.

The children's voices carried in the blue air. Then the breeze came. It cut through the branches of the trees, turning up the silver undersides of the young leaves, and brought goose bumps as it went around her. The breeze, God, the breeze! she thought. You get how many like it? Maybe a dozen in a lifetime...and already gone, down the block and picking up speed, or dying out. Either way, dead to her, and leaving in its wake a sense of excitement and mild dread. What if she failed to make the most of what remained of this perfect spring day?

She finished her wine and went inside. Jay was thumbing listlessly through the mail.

"Hey," he said.

"What should we do tonight, Jay?" she asked him.

His attention was diverted by a credit card offer. "I don't care," he said. "What do you want to do?"

"Is there anything you want to do in particular?"

"I want to do whatever you want to do," he said.

"So it's up to me to come up with something?"

He looked up from the mail at last. "You asked me to come home so we could do something."

"Because I want to do something."

"I want to do something, too," he said.

"Okay," she said, "so let's do it."

"Let's do it," he said. Then he said, "What should we do?"

She wanted to have a picnic in Central Park. They bought sandwiches from a place in the neighborhood and took the train into Manhattan. He unfurled a checkered blanket in the breeze and spread it under a tree whose canopy would have spanned half the length of their apartment. What new leaves were in ticked gently back and forth in a mild wind, like second hands on stuck clocks. She wore a shimmery green sundress with a thin white belt, slipped on quickly in the few minutes she gave them to get ready. His knees looked as pale as moons in last year's shorts. They ate their sandwiches and drank a little wine, and then they stood and tossed a Frisbee until it was just a white underbelly floating in the darkness. Before leaving, they walked into a little wooded area and with barely a sound brought each other off in two minutes with an urgency that had hibernated all winter, an urgency they both thought might have died in its hole. It was all right now; they could go home. But it was early, and he suggested going to a beer garden where they'd spent last summer drinking with friends. There was a flurry of texts and phone calls, and before too long their friends showed up—Wes and Rachel, Molly with her dog. They drank and talked until closing time. Sarah skipped ahead down the street on their way to the subway and then skipped back to him, leaping into his arms. It stayed warm through the night.

On their way into Manhattan, he told her that they had tickets to a movie that night. It was the 3-D follow-up to a superhero sequel. He had gone online the day before, only to learn that the IMAX showings were already sold out. He couldn't believe it. How far in advance did this city make IMAX tickets available for pre-purchase, and how much cunning did it take to get your hands on them? It had been such a long week, and he was tired, and, for God's sake, who thinks they need to plan more than a day in advance to see a movie? It was just a movie, it wasn't—

She put a hand out to stop him. "Jay," she said. "I'm sorry, sweets. I can't see a movie tonight."

"Why not?"

"It's so predictable," she said. "Aren't you tired of seeing movies? All we've done all winter long is go to the movies."

"But I bought the tickets already. They're bought and paid for."

"I'll reimburse you," she said. "I can't see a movie tonight."

"You're always telling me you like it when I plan things."

"It's a movie, Jay, not a weekend in Paris. I can't sit in a movie theater tonight. I'll go bonkers."

"But it doesn't start until eleven. The night's practically over by then."

"Whose night is over?" she said. "Who says the night has to be over?"

"What are you getting so excited about?" he asked.

Her focus shifted, as the train suddenly slowed to a crawl and was soon stopped altogether. Why had it stopped? They were sitting dead still in the bowels of the subway while the last hour or two—not even, not two—the last hour and change of daylight and breeze died out on the shoulders of those who had known better than to lock themselves inside the subway at such a delicate moment. Here was the underworld of the city's infinite offering: snags, delays, bottlenecks, the growing anxiety of never arriving at what was always just out of reach. It was enough to make you stand and scream and kick at the doors. Their ambitions should have been more modest. They could have walked over the Brooklyn Bridge and stopped midway to watch the sun go down.

She stood.

"Sarah?" he said.

The train started to move—not enough to jolt her but enough to get her sitting again. She didn't answer or look over.

She left the table and started toward the ladies' room of the beer garden. She walked under a sagging banner of car-lot flags weathered to white, past a bin of broken tiki torches. A thick coat of dust darkened two stacks of plastic chairs growing more cockeyed as they ascended a stucco wall. Open only a week or two after the long winter, and already the place looked defiled by a summer of rough use.

In the brig a few hours earlier, she had come to believe that in all the years she had lived in the city, this was the most temperate and gentle day it had ever conferred. Distant church bells had rung out. The blue of the sky had affected her deeply. A single cloud had drifted by like a glacier in a calm sea. Looking down, she had paid close attention to the tree nearest the brig, picking out a discrete branch. It ended in a cluster of dark nubs, ancient knuckles sheltering life. Now, breaking through, surfacing blindly to the heat and light, pale buds had begun to flower. Even here, in rusted grates, down blocks of asphalt, spring had returned. Then the breeze touched her flesh. A tingling ran down her spine to her soul, and her eyes welled with tears. Did she have a soul? In moments like this, absolutely. The breeze! She'd spent the day at her desk keeping her head down, and the snack pack convinced her it was okay—the snack pack and the energy drink, the time stolen to buy shoes online. Then this reminder, this windfall. As thrilling as a first kiss. This was her one and only life! It would require something of her to be equal to this day, she had thought at that moment in the brig, and now, looking at herself in the mirror of the ladies' room, scrutinizing her eyes—already hungover, it seemed—she had, through a series of poor choices, squandered the night drinking and failed.

She left the bathroom. Jay was everywhere surrounded by livelier tables. Their friends had not been able to come on such short notice.

"Can we go?" she asked.

She was dozing in the cab before they reached the bridge.

*   *   *

As they climbed out of the subway and the sky came into view, she knew it was too late. The ride in had taken too long and what brittle daylight remained was fast bleeding away. By the time they found food for the picnic, they would be eating in darkness.

"What are you after right now, Sarah?" Jay asked.

She saw that the streetlight was about to change. "Let's cross," she said.

"Why did I bring this stupid blanket if we're not going to the park?"

They were halfway across the street when the light went red and they found themselves marooned on an island between two-way traffic. Cars zipped by in a steady stream, giving them no room to maneuver. She turned to him.

"What should we do, Jay?"

"Oh, no," he said. "You just killed the picnic. You're in charge."

"I came up with the picnic," she said.

She needed an alternative, something to salvage this vital hour. But what? And this fucking traffic! A hundred million lights, and every one of them going against her.

"What about that one hotel?" she asked.

"Hotel?"

"You know, the one with the view."

The drinks were overpriced, and there would be no breeze, but in the lounge there was a spectacular view of Central Park. It'd be better than shopping for dinner in a badly lit bodega and having a picnic in the dark. They could always eat later.

It was a short walk. They took the elevator up. The lobby,

like the lounge, was on the thirty-fifth floor. Through the window in the distance, the park was divided in two: the westernmost trees, hunkered down beneath the tall buildings, were sunk below a line of shadow, while the rest, looking fuller, rose up in the light. The budding leaves shivered in the breeze more green than silver.

They had to wait briefly at the bar. Then the hostess came for them. Once seated in the tiered lounge, they faced outward, as in a Parisian café, and watched as the remaining trees were claimed by the shadow. They drank crisp white wine. Night settled grandly.

It still felt like winter down in the subway. There were hot gusts, weird little eddies of cold, the steel burn of brakes poisoning the platform—but never a breeze. Nothing so limpid and delicate as spring could penetrate here. Even inside the car, they were breathing last century's air. Salt tracks stained the floors. Soon winter would give way to hell: the subway's two seasons.

The train pulled into the station. The fortunate rose from their seats and stood waiting before the silver doors that failed to open. They waited and waited. Finally, off they went, given early release; two stops yet from her destination, she had more time to serve. The last of the departing passengers paraded by, and then the platform was empty, but the doors still would not close. The purgatorial train seemed to be expiring, taking in air and letting it out, pointlessly. The automated voice announced, "Ladies and gentlemen, we are being held momentarily by the train dispatcher." A ludicrous little god at play with switches.

At last the warning ding of the closing doors sounded, but

nothing happened, and the train failed to move. She was out on the edge of her seat.

She said, "I would literally rather kill myself than go to a movie tonight."

His eyes widened as if, at his desk on some Wednesday afternoon, the peal of a fire alarm had brought him to sudden life. Was she talking to him, or to herself? Her level voice was soft and frightening.

"Okay," he said. "We won't go to the movies."

Traffic eased, and at last they were free to step off the median. They hurried the rest of the way across the street. But they didn't know what to do or where to go now that the picnic was off, so they idled under the shadow of a tall building. Passersby ignored them in their push toward known destinations, fixed plans, the city's eight million souls conspiring against her joining in something urgent and mysterious.

"Sarah," he said. "Stop. Take a breath. What is it you want to do?"

"I don't know," she said. "But don't put it like that."

"Like what?"

"What *should* we do, Jay?" she said pointedly. "What *should* we do?"

"Don't they come to the same thing?"

"They don't."

She spent ten minutes searching for something on her phone. He retreated a few feet, squatting near a scrawny tree planted in a little cell. When she gestured, he rose to his feet and followed her, keeping a step behind. At the next corner, they waited as taxis bounced by on their shocks. They caught every red light thereafter. They reached the building she wanted, the one with the lounge with a view of the park. She kept hitting the button as the elevator made its way down to them.

They were the last ones out when the doors opened. The window just past the reception area showed the buildings down Fifty-Ninth Street checkerboarded with lights in the dimming hour. Bankers in their brigs, she thought. A canopy of shadow was slowly rolling across the treetops, sinking everything into a silver night.

There were no tables available. The hostess took Jay's name.

"Should we be here?" Sarah asked him.

"Isn't this where you wanted to be?"

The hostess watched them. "You're welcome to sit at the bar," she told them.

"Thank you."

"How long until a table is free?" Sarah asked.

The hostess didn't know. She couldn't guarantee one at all.

They went to the bar, where they drank in silence.

She had wanted a picnic, then the subway had defeated her. Then they'd been stranded on the median bickering over nothing, the all-consuming nothing of what to do. Was it she, she alone, who made that question so inscrutable and accusing some nights, like a stranger leveling a finger at her from across a room? Or was it the haltings and blinders of an entwined life: the fact of Jay, the disequilibrium of having to take what he wanted into consideration, whatever that might be? Because he kept it to himself, or it remained alien to him, and so how could she hope to name it? Or maybe there was no mystery at all. Maybe he was just a man who wanted to see a movie.

The last of the daylight disappeared as they waited, and all the possibility that had arrived with the breeze was reduced to yet another series of drinks at a bar. By the time a table opened up, she felt drunk and unfocused. They had a final drink and left.

They tried having dinner at a cheap Italian joint downtown, but they got into a fight and left before he would even enter the restaurant. When they got home, they were no longer speaking. They lay in the dark for a long time before he broke the silence. "I could have gone to a fucking movie," he said. He rolled over and went to sleep.

At the bottom of the subway stairs, she reached for him, turned, and, with his hand in hers, raced back the way they'd come, up the stairs, into the mellow night. She breathed the spring air in deeply, shedding the subway stuff, and the still-blue sky above them confirmed her good judgment. But he was confused.

"I thought we were having a picnic."

"Let's not get on the subway," she said. "I can't stand it down there, not right now. Let's just walk."

"Walk where?"

She led him west toward the Brooklyn Bridge. On the pedestrian walkway, she skipped ahead, then waited for him, then skipped ahead again, swung around and smiled. They came to a stop midway between Manhattan and Brooklyn just as the sun was setting. The wavelets in the bay turned over in little strokes, scaling the water silver before it darkened to stone. She looked straight up. Just to see the towering spires of the bridge climbing to a single point in the sky was to affirm that nothing more could be asked of this hour, nothing better apprehended in this life. She took hold of a steel cable in each hand and gazed out again at the setting sun. The burn-off against the buildings grew milder, its colors deeper; for a minute, the certainty that it would die out was in doubt. Then the sun dropped away, and a blue shadow settled over everything—the bridge, the water. It mirrored the cool ferric touch of the suspension cables. She let go, and the blood came back to her hands in heavy pulses. Her eyes filled with tears.

When the last of the sunlight was gone, she turned to him and said, "What did you think of that?"

He looked at her with perfect innocence. "Of what?" he said.

They waited a long time for their drinks to arrive. The bar was situated—stupidly, to her mind—far from the view, and besides, they sat with their backs to it. They had nothing to stare at but liquor bottles and wineglasses, while outside the sun was disappearing and shadow was unfurling swiftly across the trees.

It had been a terrible idea to come up here, thinking they'd fall miraculously into a table. She wanted the city to be full of exclusive places turning people away, as long as it always accommodated her. It didn't work like that. What a stupid place to live—stretched thin, overbooked, sold out in advance. And, as if choosing the wrong place weren't bad enough, there were all those alternatives, abstractions taking shape only now: a walk across the bridge, drinks with Molly at the beer garden. Lights, crowds, parties. Even staying put in the brig, watching the neighborhood descend into darkness. Oh, God, was it possible... the best way to have spent the night was to never have left the brig?

Knees pressed up against the bar, she turned to him as best she could. "I'm sorry, Jay," she said.

"For what?"

"For rushing us out of the apartment, and for how I acted on the subway. And it was a mistake to come up here. Let's do something," she said.

"Okay," he said. "Like what?"

The second he asked, the desire came over her to be in the park, obscured by trees, bent over, her fingertips dug into the earth, as he pushed her panties down to her ankles. In her mind they wouldn't be perfectly concealed, so he would feel rushed and as a result would be rough with her, dispensing with the considerate sheets-and-pillow concerns of their weekend sex life to fuck her, simply fuck her hard and fast. Then the passersby with their exciting plans could ignore them all they wanted. She'd feel no sense of exclusion then. She'd right herself as he was buckling up, straighten her sundress, smile at him, and, just like that, all the stale tenement air of married life would disperse.

"Sounds like you have something in mind, Sarah," he said, taking her hand under the bar. "Tell me what it is."

Do it, she dared herself. Just lean in and whisper it.

"I'm up for anything," he said.

But she lost the nerve.

"I don't really know," she said. "What do you want to do?"

He suggested they buy their sandwiches for the picnic from the neighborhood place before getting on the train. But no, God, please no, not the neighborhood place again! She was so sick of it. They had lived off that menu for as long as she could remember. Then she climbed out of the subway and knew they'd made a mistake. Finding food would take forever. But if she called off the picnic because there was no time to find food, then what did they have if not time? Time to squander and squander until the night was over. One night after another until a whole life flew by. The first day of spring could make her go a little crazy, start thinking her options were either a picnic or death. Jay was charging forward, blanket under his arm, toward the picnic he believed was still on, when she stopped. It took him a minute to notice. He turned, then walked slowly back to her.

It wasn't in him to see what made this day different from other days. He didn't pick up on breezes and breaks in weather, or they came upon him as the natural course of things, and so what was the big deal? If he had had his druthers, even today he would have worked into the night, feeding at his desk from some Styrofoam trough, then hurried to meet her for the late-night showing of the 3-D follow-up to the superhero sequel. Once home, he would have collapsed on the bed as if all the adventurous excursions of the day had depleted him of everything but the delicious aftertaste of exhaustion. She wanted to be a different person, a better person, but he was perfectly happy being his limited self.

She had made a series of bad decisions, and now she traced them back to their source. It was not forgoing the sandwiches, or stepping onto the subway, or heading into Manhattan at the wrong hour. It was not leaving the brig, where she had fallen into a fragile harmony with the day. It was asking Jay to come home early. That was the mistake that had set everything else in motion.

"What is it?" he asked.

She was about to tell him. She had overcome her fear and was about to tell him everything when she said, "Thanks for carrying the blanket."

He looked at the blanket in his hands. "Sure," he said.

Darkness fell. They bought food and carried on into the park. She could see vaguely that it was him as they laid everything out on the blanket, but when the time came to pack up, it was so dark that he could have been anyone, and she was grateful.

Night drew more people out of doors and into the beer garden, and one by one the chairs climbing the stucco wall in two tilting stacks were dispersed around twenty or so patio tables. Molly showed up late with Chester, her golden retriever, and had nowhere to sit. Sarah stood and kissed her oldest friend, telling her to take her seat while she ran inside; she'd bring another chair back with her on her return from the bathroom. Chester, a lazy dog, quickly dropped his paws and began panting at his owner's feet, but Molly was up again in no time when she spotted Sarah returning. Only Sarah didn't return. She walked through the wrought-iron trellis and out of the beer garden.

"Jay," she said. "Where's Sarah going?"

Sarah was a block away by the time Jay caught up with her.

"Where are you going, Sarah? Why are you leaving?"

"It's over, Jay!" she cried. "It's over!"

"What's over?" he said.

She stopped resisting and swiveled to face him. Passersby, intrigued by the sight of another life on fire, skirted around them and turned back to stare.

She didn't have the heart to tell him. "Spring," she said.

"What do you mean it's over, Sarah? Spring just started."

But he was wrong. Spring was a fleeting moment and it blew right past her like that breeze on the brig. Then summer rushed in, as hot and oppressive as pipe exhaust, and she just couldn't take another summer in the city. It would be followed by another single moment, that cool instant the leaves changed color. Then it would be winter again, another interminable winter, each one endured and misspent until they accrued into a life whose final hour she would never be ready to face.

"Tell me you get it, Jay," she said. "Please tell me you get it." She leaned her head into his chest. "I'm scared to death," she said.

"What just happened?" he asked. "What went wrong?"

"What are we doing? Why did we come here?"

"Where?"

"What else could we have done?"

"We did a lot," he said. "We had a picnic. Now we're with friends. Why are you so upset?"

"Should I not do the thing I do?" she asked. "Or should I do the thing I don't do?"

"What thing are you talking about?" he asked.

He went back to the beer garden to say goodbye to their friends and to reassure them that everything was okay. But when he returned to the corner, she was already in a cab on her way into Brooklyn. She gathered a few things from the apartment—her pills, her toiletries—and an hour later she was in Molly's apartment telling her friend her marriage was over.

*　　*　　*

The hostess who had invited them to wait at the bar now came for them, just in time to quash another dumb argument before it got out of hand, and led them to a table in the lounge. The frustrations on the subway, the dithering on the street, the self-doubt, all was forgotten before the stunning view. Even as the light was draining away and the trees outside the tall window were sinking into darkness, it was impossible not to feel restored. And with drinks on their way, and the night still young, she could sit in peace a moment without making any sudden moves from the terror of being in the wrong place doing the wrong thing.

"What do you think?" Jay asked her. "Happy?"

"Yes."

"Good," he said.

He did want her to be happy. And she could be so very unfair, expecting too much from them both on any given night and then going out of her mind when they came up short, blaming everything on him, the bickering, the bad decisions. He wasn't to blame. He wasn't a bad man. Only a little dull. Look at him now, spurning the view to focus on his domestic bottle of beer, pick-pick-picking at the label with his fingertips. That was no reason to wonder why she had married him, or to contemplate setting a divorce in motion and starting over. She knew herself well enough to know that the happiness she sought, so much like relief from pain, would not be handed to her by a partner, even one more passionate and alive to the possibilities than Jay, but was something she had to find on her own. It was the want of her own daring that haunted her. Overcome that, and Jay had always been game to do whatever she wished.

"Jay?"

"Hmmm," he said.

"Look at me."

He looked up from his beer, though he continued to pick.

"Know what I've always wanted to do?"

"What's that?"

"In the park? Behind some trees?"

"What?"

"Lean in, Jay. Let me whisper it in your ear."

The hostess never rescued them. The view of the park remained out of sight. The bar where their knees touched never turned comfortable, and they left.

"Well, that was a bust," Jay remarked helpfully on the elevator ride down.

The street again. Only difference now: it was dark. Half the night was over. Stupid to think that when it wasn't yet eight o'clock, but she couldn't help it. The past hour of frustrations and bad luck, of vacillating, of stalling out at a moment in time when she needed the most to happen, had come to define her night, and her life.

"What are you in the mood for?" he asked.

"Whatever," she said.

"Dinner?"

"Sure."

"Dinner, or not?"

"I said sure."

"Not with any conviction."

"What do you want from me, Jay?"

"The night's not over, you know."

"Let's go to dinner."

"Here, or downtown?"

"Either way."

"Sarah."

"Downtown. Downtown. Downtown."

They took a cab downtown. That was the most they could imagine for themselves on this first night of spring: another dinner downtown. Food was the default, food and alcohol, whenever the imagination failed. They would eat and drink themselves sick and call that, somehow, living.

On the corner of Delancey and Allen, she stepped out of the cab, over a puddle and onto the curb at the same instant that a group of friends in a rowdy mood burst through the door of a bar. She didn't know them. She hardly had time to register them. But she knew at once that she wanted to be in the thick of *that* night, and not this lame one where she and her husband went to dinner again and drank too much out of sheer boredom.

Jay paid the cabbie and met her at the corner. "Do you have a taste for something in particular?"

"No."

They went down the block, stopping here and there to read a menu. "What do you think of this place?" he asked.

"It's fine."

"You're not crazy about it."

"Do I have to be crazy about it? It's dinner, who cares. It's fine."

"It should be more than fine if we're going to drop a hundred bucks in there," he said. "It should be a place you want to go."

"Oh, for fuck's sake," she said, and opened the door and walked inside.

It was an Italian place with checkered tablecloths, guaranteed to be nothing special. And air-conditioned! Who runs an air conditioner on the first day of spring? It was an affront to time. This place had the most delicate day of the year in a chokehold, waiting for its legs to stop kicking. There'd be no limpid breeze here, only a cheap blast of recycled air. She'd have turned and walked out had Jay been beside her, but she'd scored some obscure point against him out on the street just now and wasn't ready to forfeit it.

She followed the hostess to a table in the far back. Jay was still hanging in the window, refusing to come inside—unbelievable! She opened the menu to ignore him. So this, finally, was what the night had come down to: a squalid little showdown at a cheap Italian restaurant that was as far from a picnic in the park as—

She didn't see him open the door. He raised his voice above the racket.

"I'm not fucking eating in there!" he yelled.

Startled, she watched him disappear as the door fell slowly shut. People turned. She was mortified. Stared at, cast out, or feeling so, she stood and walked toward the door, aware as she hadn't been on the way in that Jay had picked out the perfect place. The traditional tablecloths enlivened by the roar of conversation and ringing laughter. Everyone in perfect little parties of friends and lovers. Not a soul burdened by the possibility of a different night, better companions, competing visions of a finer life, as their nourishment arrived at the table like destiny.

She had found the nerve to whisper into her husband's ear, and by some miracle Jay ceased picking at his bottle of beer and could not call for the check fast enough.

Seems he, too, wanted to break out of the missionary rut, he just didn't know how to suggest it. He lacked the initiative of other men, their imagination, or maybe just their daring. Well, at least he was game. That was half the battle.

In the elevator he looked over at her with a suggestive, un-inhibited, private smile she hadn't seen in months, and already it seemed they were renewed.

"Is this what you had planned for us all along?" he asked. "Is this why you asked me to come home early?"

No, she hadn't planned it. She had asked him to come home only to make something like it possible. But she didn't tell him that.

They entered the park at Fifty-Ninth and Columbus, threaded their way through the last of the runners and cyclists on the inner drive, and walked north along a winding footpath until darkness fell completely. At Strawberry Fields they hopped a fence and slipped behind some bushes.

If, in her fantasy, which apparently took place in late summer, they weren't perfectly concealed, there had certainly been more leaves! They seemed to be so very out in the open still. Was that a woman going by with a stroller? Foreplay was out, a luxury they couldn't afford. He unbuckled in a hurry. She had to take her panties down herself.

She was bent over, waiting.

"Do you need help?" she asked.

"Shh...do you hear that?"

"What?"

He was quiet.

"Jay?"

"I need some help," he said.

She turned to help. A few minutes later, she brought her hands back to the ground. She waited.

"I lost it," he said.

She stood and dusted the dirt from her hands.

"That's okay," she said. He was quickly buckling up. She reached out and touched him on the head.

There was an essential difference between them—what he might have called her restlessness, what she might have called his complacency—which had not surfaced before they were married, or, if it had, only as a hint of things to come, hidden again as soon as it peeked out. When they argued now, as a married couple, it was often over this essential difference. Why could she not be more like him and why could he not be more like her? But if there was some intractable self in her that was so easy to identify and so deserving of scorn, it was one in search of more life, more adventure, of the right thing to do at any given hour. It was not a homebody. It was not a moviegoer.

But suddenly she stopped. Was she really any less predictable than she accused him of being? Night after night she was anxious not to miss out on... what? She didn't know. Something she couldn't define, forever residing just out of reach. It must get to be so tiresome for him, she thought. He must be convinced by now that she would never find it, that indeed there was nothing to find.

She was no longer beside him. It took him a minute to notice. He turned, then walked slowly back to her.

She reached out and took his hand. "Jay," she said. "What do you want to do tonight?"

"I thought we were having a picnic."

"But that was my idea," she said. "What do *you* want?"

"I want to have a picnic," he said.

"Am I predictable, Jay? Am I tiresome? I must drive you nuts."

"Because you like picnics?"

He put his arm around her, and they walked the rest of the way to the park. Friends again. Was it so hard? After they ate, they lay on the blanket in the dark and talked for the first time about starting a family.

He was gloomy on the ride downtown, and gloomy when they stepped out of the cab. Gloomy going from restaurant to restaurant while she studied the menus posted outside.

"Do you have a taste for anything in particular?"

"No," he said.

"Do you just want to go home?"

"Whatever," he said. "Up to you."

"Well, I don't want to go home," she said.

She chose a harmless Italian place. She wanted to turn to him to express her outrage that they were blasting the air-conditioning on the first day of spring, but she knew that he wasn't in the mood.

The place was louder than she expected, a fate that became clear only after they'd been seated. They looked at the menu, keeping their impressions to themselves. Finally, he set his down on the checkered tablecloth, on top of the blanket he'd brought for the picnic.

"Do you know what you're getting?"

He shrugged.

"Jay," she said, "it doesn't matter, it really doesn't."

"Maybe not to you," he said.

"I'm sorry that I even suggested it," she said.

"Why did you touch my head?" he asked.

"What?"

"Afterwards," he said. "Did you really have to pat me on the head?"

She returned to studying the menu. Had she patted him? She hadn't meant to. She was just trying to make him feel better. When she looked up, sometime later, she found Jay staring intently across the room. She tracked his gaze to a table and to the man there who was, she thought, his opposite in every way: charismatic at a glance, holding the table rapt with some expansive conversation. He was the handsomest man in New York, no doubt about it. A man like that would know what to do with her in the park. Jay's fixation on him, she thought, while sullen and violent with envy, was also, possibly, at root, pure curiosity, a reflection, a desire. He wanted to be the man, or at least someone like him: someone poised, commanding, rapacious. He would never change, but, in his way, he wanted to, as she had always wanted most to be someone better than she was.

They waited for their meal in silence, in muted unhappiness, the odd ones out in that lively place. They ate quickly, but it took forever. She just kept drinking. She stuffed herself with food and wine, and though she considered opening the door on the way home and throwing herself from the cab, she fell asleep instead, which by then sort of, if not entirely, came to the same thing.

He went to bed when they got home. She stepped out on the brig. She was too dulled to respond to any breeze now, and she understood that her night had ended several hours earlier, just as she believed it was beginning, when everything she was seeking from the world had been brought out from within her.

They missed out on a picnic. The park was a bust. And dinner just made them feel dull. When eleven o'clock rolled around, they found themselves standing in line outside the movie theater. The night was practically over by then anyway.

"You sure you want to do this?" he asked.

"Why wouldn't I be?"

"You said earlier that you'd rather kill yourself than go to the movies tonight."

"Well, that was then."

"And what's now?"

"Now it doesn't matter," she said.

They went inside and watched the 3-D follow-up to the superhero sequel. It made Jay very happy. Then they went home and went to bed.

"In the brig!" she called out.

With her wineglass at a tilt, she peered down again on the neighborhood. Two boys in bike helmets rode their scooters past the stoop where their mothers sat. Someone unseen was sweeping a broom rhythmically across a courtyard. Then the breeze came. It was mellow, carrying off the last of winter, and transformed inside her into a warm chill that ran down her spine to her soul. What a breeze! You didn't get too many like it. It reminded her that time was ticking down, that life was for the taking, and that if she failed to seize the hour it would be gone forever. She hurried inside to Jay, who was idly flipping through the mail.

"Hey," he said, without looking up.

She set her wineglass down. What did she need wine for? She removed the credit card offer from his hand, and he looked at her at last.

"Come outside with me, Jay," she said, taking him by the hand. "There's a nice breeze out there. I wouldn't want you to miss it."

Ghost Town Choir

One day Lawton was with us at the picnic and the next day he was outside the trailer with his boom box singing "What Have You Got Planned Tonight, Diana." That is not a good song. She was trying to ignore him, but he was outside with his foot up on a milk crate, and he was singing. She was doing what she does whenever she's mad at me—cleaning everything in sight and banging the pots and pans around. Then she stopped at the sink and stuck her middle finger up at Lawton in the window, and the look on her face said it was the end of good times. *What have you got planned tonight, Diana?* he sang, though my mom's name is Sheryl. *Would you consider lying in my arms?* "He doesn't give a *fuck* what I have planned," she said to me. "He just wants his records back." I didn't know what was happening, but I was guessing it was all over with Lawton. She was having me collect the dirty dishes. I was finding them everywhere, with stuff on them I couldn't even remember eating. Old bowls of oatmeal, and spoons covered in peanut butter. "What is this, Bob, a spatula? How many times do I have to tell you? You can't let these things sit." "Mom, why are you mad at Lawton?" She opened the window above the sink, and all her figurines fell into the water. "Because I got an expiration date on my stupidity!" she yelled out at him. Then she went to the door and started throwing things. The Ball jars, the butter knives. People were peering out from their windows and door-ways, but only for, like, a murder does anyone on Stock Island ever call the police. Lawton was laughing, showing his buck-teeth. His mustache moved up and down like a centipede. He was watching the kitchen things whiz by him until the time he turned back and got pinged on the collarbone with an I ♥ Florida mug. He quit singing like *that,* picked up his boom box and stomped away.

After that, she put on her big blue plastic gloves and started in on the bathroom. She hadn't cleaned in about six months, ever since she broke up with the cop. "I'm sick of throwing away men's combs," she said, throwing away Lawton's comb in one of those huge lawn-care trash bags. "I'm beginning to believe a free comb is about all they have to offer." She also threw away a toothbrush and some hair tonic. When she got to the toilet bowl, she said, "I'll be happy when it's just your hairs and my hairs again, Bob. There's nothing nastier than a man's hairs." "I don't have hairs," I said. "You have head hairs," she said. "And I love every single one of them." She mussed my hair up with the blue gloves on, which was kind of gross. Then she went back to cleaning. "But can you think of a single man worth these hairs?" she asked, turning the sponge over and showing me all the hairs from the toilet on it. "The cop," I said. "The cop?" she said. "How do you even remember the cop?" "I don't know," I said. "Only thing I remember about the cop was that he wasn't worth a single one of these hairs," she said. She ran the sponge under the water. "What about Lawton?" I asked. "Oh, Bob," she said. "You have about the same good taste in men as I do. How could you like Lawton?" "He has good arm veins," I said. "And he was a cowboy." She stopped cleaning. "What ever made him a cowboy?" "His card," I said, "from the Cowboy Hall of Fame. I've seen it. He keeps it in his wallet." "Let me tell you something," she said. She stopped cleaning and took her gloves off. She got on her knees and took hold of my arms. "There's three things that man's done in his life approximating success. He kicked dope, one. He won a paternity suit. And he switched to low-tar. Those are his three achievements. Sure as shit he's no cowboy."

She got off her knees and went into the main room, even though the bathroom still wasn't but half-clean. She lifted up the sofa cushions and pulled out three quarters, two fish sticks and a bottle of baby aspirin. She pocketed the quarters. Everything else she put in the trash bag. "I swear to God, Bob," she said to me. "I don't know why I pay you an allowance. What is it you do around here—anything?" She shook an enormous tube sock at me. "Can't you at least put your stuff away?" "That's not mine," I said. "I don't have that big a foot." She considered the tube sock again before putting it in the bag. She hated that trailer. She hated how small it was. Whenever she got a ball of fire up her butt to clean, she dumped everything into the trash, no matter what. That's how it was with Lawton's records. There was a whole milk crate full. "You can't throw those away," I said to her. She swiveled around on me so fast. "Why do you stick up for him, huh, Bob? Why stick up for a man who won't even throw a Frisbee with you at a picnic on account of the schedule of beer he's trying to keep to?" "Mom, you can't throw those away," I said. "They're his whole life." She dumped them all in. "Then there's no better place for them than the trash," she said.

When she returned from the dumpsters, she didn't go back to cleaning. She did something she's never done before. She put on her tool belt and got down on her knees with about a hundred tools, and soon her sweaty bangs were sticking to her forehead like they do when she's cleaning. "Mom!" I said. "What are you doing?" "What's it look like I'm doing?" she asked. "I'm taking up this old floor." And she was, too. She was tearing it up strip by strip. "But that's the floor!" I said. "I'm sick of this old floor, Bob," she said. "Aren't you? Look at it. It's all brown." "So?" She swept the back of her wrist across her forehead to get the sweat off. "Just look around you, Bob. Everything's so fucking brown. Aren't you sick of it?" I didn't know what she meant other than the TV and the lamp shades, and the fridge, and the walls and the carpet. I guess I'd never noticed just how much brown there was all around us. "How come you don't like brown?" I asked. She pulled really hard with some kind of gripper tool and tore another strip of floor like it was taffy all the way to the carpet. Then she sat back on her knees.

"Brown is the color of men," she said. She started to count off on her fingers. "Brown teeth. Brown smiles. Brown mustaches. Brown penises swinging all over the place, standing up to say hi under the brown sheets. I'm sick of those fucking sheets," she said. "They're going, too. We're starting all over again with whites at the Walmart."

She was still pulling up the floor when I got bored. "Mom,

can I have something to eat?" I asked. "Take my purse and go up to the Citgo," she said. I moaned. "I'm so sick of hot dogs," I said. "They got burritos, don't they?" "I'm sick of damn burritos." "Hey, watch it, mister," she said. She didn't like me cussing, even though she cussed all the time. "How come you didn't want to marry Lawton?" I asked. "Marry Lawton!" she cried. She whooped at that. "Marry Lawton!" "But how come?" "Because of the astrological charts, Bob." "Be serious, Mom," I said. "Let me tell you why I didn't marry Lawton," she said. "Because I'm a bitch, and he's a son of a bitch, and the two never go well together. Now go get my purse, and you can run up to the Citgo and get yourself something to eat." "Do you think he's a good fiddler, at least?" She was just squatting there, staring at the refrigerator. "I never heard him play the fiddle," she said. "Now go get my purse." I came back with it, and she rummaged around, looking for loose change for my burrito but pulling out her makeup instead. "What about his singing voice?" I asked. "What about it?" She found some lipstick, put it on, and mushed her lips together. "Do you think he's a good singer?" "That's all Lawton ever did was sing a sad song," she said. She put the lipstick back in her purse and set the purse on the counter. Then she pulled the two quarters she found under the sofa cushion out from her pocket and gave them to me. "Did you like it when he sang to you, at least?" "He didn't sing *to* me, Bob. He just sang." "But did you like it?" She was still staring at the fridge. She sighed real heavy. "It was about the worse voice you ever heard," she said, "but I guess you could still call it singing."

I took my two quarters and went outside, but instead of going to the Citgo, I went down to the dumpsters and pulled out Lawton's records. I had my crappy red wagon with me, the one with the wobbly wheels that I had to pull with a rope because the handle was broke. I lined all of Lawton's records up real snug on the wagon and pulled them past the playground that was still under water from the last hurricane, over the chicken bones and cigarette butts that were mixed in with the wood chips, and into the forest. It wasn't a real forest, just like a hundred trees. That was where my fort was. I took everything down there: belts, aftershave, tube socks, old pocketknives, packs and packs of cigarettes. Anything anybody ever left behind. She'd say, "I'm beginning to think a half a pack of cigarettes is all they have to offer." Did they know about the cigarettes they'd never smoke? Did they ever dream they'd end up down here at my fort? Sometimes I'd put on their old aftershave, forget all about it, and when she came home from work, she'd sniff at the air and say, "Did somebody stop by today?"

Inside my fort, I looked through his records. The one on top was called *Ghost Town Choir,* by Bluford Tucker and the Abandon Boys. I knew that one. It was Lawton's favorite.

Her boy come by after she threw that mug at me and I got to holler at him from the sofa. "You cain't come around here no more, boy!" "But how come?" he says. "I like it down here." "I don't care," I tell him. "Go on, sing it somewhere else." Then, don't even ask—just climbs the two cinder block stairs and enters the trailer. I got to remind myself to put a door on. "You not hear me, boy?" I have more than once expressed to his mama the need for a restraint of some kind, be it medical or an old-fashioned collar. He's holding something behind his back, and when he brings it out real proud and happy, you'd think he had himself a gold seal on the Ten Commandments. "What you got there?" I ask. It's one of my old 45s his mama's been hoarding from me on account of her spite and damnation. *Ghost Town Choir* by somebody called Bluford Tucker. Tell the truth, I don't much listen to music anymore. But his mama's got a real advantage on me, not giving them records back. So I nod a bit to show him he's done good, trying to recall that Bluford Tucker sound and drawing a blank. Hillbilly music, in all likelihood, but I'd have to give it a spin to recollect it proper. Just never too sure where that old player is around here. I take it out anyways, as if to inspect it for scratches and whatnot, and sure enough that's when I see there ain't no sleeve. "Where's the sleeve?" I ask him. He acquires that look, the one his mama wears when I talk music, that says "I don't speak music." "See, now—all my records have plastic sleeves. Keeps them from getting scratched all to hell. Now where's this one's sleeve?" He don't say a damn thing. "Has your mama been fucking with my sleeves?" "I don't think so," he says. "You know how important this album is to me, boy?" He nods like he does know. He ain't got a fucking clue. Music is what I'd call a highlight in an otherwise low life. What's the point of going on without your damn music? "You know what this means," I say to him. "I guess she never really loved me, your mama." Seems the right moment to drift off and lick my wounds, but there ain't enough room in this goddamn trailer for that. So he says, "How come you and my mom broke up?" He's got the one talent in life, and that's making people talk. "What makes you say we broke up?" I ask him. "Didn't you?" "Well, I guess it's true she didn't like the way I was treating you at that picnic." "How were you treating me?" "I didn't treat you any which way," I tell him. "But you ask her, I wasn't treating you like I was your daddy. Well, you know what, son? I ain't nobody's daddy. You see?" He goes quiet, but you can see him calculating. "So . . . you broke up because of me?" Now see that? That's that boy for you, right there. You don't even recollect taking a seat down next to him, but when you look up, there you are. "It's more than that, boy. It's a way of looking at things, and your mama and me, we ain't ever seen one thing that looked the same." "But you liked her, though, didn't you? Didn't you like her?" "Things about her I liked." "Like what?" "She could drink a beer now and then. I liked that about her." "What else?" "She was a roofer. You don't find too many lady roofers. Liked when she'd come home in that pair of knee pads." "I want you to tell me something and be honest," he says. "Did you love my mom, or didn't you?" "Now how can I love a woman who's hoarding all my record albums?" I ask him. "You know what them record albums mean to me? They're just about my whole damn life." "What if she gave them all back to you?" he asks.

What the boy don't know is how awful happy I was to be taking them down there in the first place. I was wanting his mama and me to make a night of it. She had one of them players on top of her tape deck/radio. Boy was there, too. We all listened. It was real home-like. Not bad, I thought, not bad at all. I should try, I thought, I really should. Why not? She's got that player. Player works. Why not? Could have us some more nice nights like that one. It didn't come to that, though. Nope, came to something else. And now it'd be a shame to have them back. Don't listen to them myself. Ain't had a player in a hundred years. Don't give a good goddamn about music anymore.

I get them records back, they'd be another reminder that it was all over and nothing more to talk about.

So I give Bluford Tucker back to him and tell him I don't want it. Tell him take it back down to his mama. "But why?" he says. "I thought you said you wanted them. Don't you want them?" "Not one at a time, I don't. I want all of 'em at once or none at all." "But if she gave them all back, you wouldn't have any reason to come by anymore." "Ain't you been hearing her, boy? She don't want me coming by. She don't want to have a damn thing to do with me." "But she does!" he cries. "She likes the way you sing! Don't you know that? She thinks you have a good singing voice." "Does she now," I say. And you almost want to believe him, the way he nods his head. "She tell you that?" He nods again. "Won't you come back?" he says. "Come back just one more time," he says. "The two of you can make up, I know you can. And then you can get your records back." "You think so, do you?" "I know so," he says. "I know it for a fact."

And would you look at that? He's got me talking again, talking and thinking. I reach out and lift him up by the scrawny arms.

"Your mama and me, boy, we're done. I'm sorry to say it, but that's what happens when a man gets tangled up with a woman. Shit gets lost. Sometime it's things, and sometimes it's people." I carefully deposit his ass directly outside the trailer. "Say you were her cousin, I might allow you to be down here from time to time, providing you had beer. But she shit in her own nest when she had you, and I cain't stand the smell of it. So go on, get out."

* * *

When I came back from Lawton's I was super hungry because I never made it to the Citgo, so I opened the fridge for some cheese slices and my hand came back all wet and cold. The whole fridge was painted white! I couldn't believe it. I looked at it up close. I guess it had been brown before. It still looked a little brown because the old color was coming through. "Mom," I said. "Did you paint the fridge?" She turned and saw my handprint on the door handle. "Oh, Bob!" she cried. "Now look what you've done! I just finished with that two seconds ago." She got the paintbrush from the sink and smoothed out the handle. There were still lots of drips everywhere. "Why'd you paint the fridge?" I asked. "Because I got sick of putting our food in a cold turd," she said. "But can you do that to the fridge?" "I guess I can," she said. "Last time I checked it was our fridge." "But why paint it?" "Don't you ever want just a little change, Bob? Huh? Even if it's just a color? Just some stupid little change?" "Are you ever going to fix the floor?" I asked her. "It's only been a few hours, Bob. I'm working on it." "This place is a mess," I said. "Hey," she said. "You don't like it, you can go live somewhere else."

We both heard Lawton at the same time. "Sheryl Lynn!" he yelled from outside. "I want my records back, goddamn it! Give me my goddamn records!" We just stared at each other. Then I went to the window and she went to the door. He started calling her all sorts of names, like slut and bitch and cunt and whore. She turned around, grabbed food from the cabinets, and started throwing it at him. Boxes of spirals and cheese at first, and packages of microwave popcorn. But then a can of Campbell's soup. It landed in the gravel, and he got mad. "Stop your throwing, Sheryl Lynn! It ain't right what you're doing, putting that boy between me and you. You just hand over all them records and I'll be on my way." "Don't pretend you give a damn about this boy!" she cried. "You can't even be bothered to throw a Frisbee with him at a picnic, you piece of shit!" She hauled a jar of pickle relish at him, and even though he ducked, it came real close to hitting him on the head. He picked up my bat after that. A Louisville Slugger. I kept it leaning up against the trailer. "I like that boy, Sheryl Lynn," he said. "But I told you already. I ain't his daddy. So what I do at a picnic ain't nobody's business but my own." She threw a two-liter bottle of soda at him, and he hit it with the bat. Soda went everywhere. "Goddamn it, Sheryl Lynn!" he said. "Stop it, now! What'd I tell you? I ain't ever doing to your boy what my daddy did to me! Never never never never never! If you only knew—good Lord, girl, you should be grateful. You should, Sheryl Lynn. I swear to God you should. So just give me my records back and let me be!" "I threw all of your stupid old records in the trash!" she screamed. "Every single one of them! Exactly where they belong—and where *you* belong!" I thought for sure he was going to come inside and swing at her when he heard that. But instead, he dropped the bat and fell to his knees. "Oh, take me back, Sheryl Lynn!" he cried out to her. "Honey darling, please!" he said. "Don't you see I'm just begging you, darling? Give me just one more chance!" But I guess she didn't want to, because she just kept throwing stuff, like refried beans, and a half-full bottle of dish soap, screaming, "Go fuck yourself!" I couldn't take it anymore. "Please stop!" I yelled. "Please don't fight! I got your records, Lawton! They're down at my fort! I'll take you there! I'll give them back!" He got up off his knees. I guess I thought it was all over after that. He'd go down to the fort with me, and I'd give him his records back. But before I could walk out of the trailer, he took hold of that Louisville Slugger again and started swinging. He hit the potted plants that hung from the trailer, and the cans of white paint that my mom had used to paint the fridge. He didn't stop swinging until dirt and paint were everywhere. Then he dropped that bat and walked home.

Few hours later, that boy come by carrying something in a garbage bag on a wagon real careful-like so as not to let it spill over. I see it all from the window. I feign business when he comes up to the door, just me and my magazine. He don't so much as step foot on the first stair when I got no choice but to notice him. "Well, don't just stand there in a man's doorway," I tell him. "That's liable to get you shot." First time he don't just come on in, even with an invitation. He takes up that garbage bag instead and gives it the heave-ho. It lands just inside the trailer there, and I see it for what it is, a stretched-out thing full of record albums. He stands in the doorway making ready to leave. "Well, you're here," I say. "Might as well come in." "I can't," he says. "Get in here, boy," I say.

It takes him a while, but eventually he has a seat next to me.

"Brought me my records, did you?" He nods. "That's a good man," I tell him. "A man can't do without his music."

He's an unhappy boy. Life's made him that way, life and his time of life. There's nothing working out for him and everything a frustration. What he needs is a daddy. I could use a daddy myself. Hell, who couldn't use a daddy? "I'm sorry I couldn't be more of a help to you, boy. Honest to God I am. But if you only knew. You'd be grateful. You truly would." "Can I see your wallet?" he says to me. "My wallet? What do you want with that for?" "Can I?" he says. I consider it. "If it's my wallet you want," I tell him, "it can't be my fortune you're after." So I dig it out and hand it to him. He opens it up and points. "Can I have this?" he asks.

It's my daddy's Cowboy Hall of Fame card. Those record albums, what do I care about them? Music's all over and done with. But that card, that's an honest-to-God card right there. Only thing I ever got from that man, and not exactly something I care to part with.

But I guess it's like I told the boy. Shit gets lost.

"Take it," I tell him. "But then we're even. And I don't ever want to see you down here ever again."

For as long as I can remember, my mom drove a two-door Ford Pinto with a brown exterior she called "shit brown." The body was marred by many dents big and small. The hood was warped, which meant the car rattled over even the slightest uneven ground. The red engine light never went off. The legend of a backward-bucking horse branded the glove box and the floor mats. I spent as much time searching that car's nooks and crannies for loose change as I did riding from place to place in the passenger seat. She hated that car more than anything, and when I got home that day from Lawton's, it was gone. Just gone. The world is stable until it isn't, and afterward there is no going back.

She was waiting for me out front, sitting inside a white pickup truck with blue racing stripes. I didn't even see her. I was heading inside when she said, "Don't go in there, Bob." It startled me. "I made a hash of things in there," she said. "Just get in." I went up to her at the window. "What are you doing in that truck?" I asked. "This is our truck now," she said. "Do you like it?" "Where's our car?" "I made the man a trade," she said. "I thought we'd be more like cowboys in a pickup truck. And I know how much you like cowboys." "You got rid of the car?" "I was sick of that car," she said. "I made a good trade. Now come on, get in." I went around the back of the truck. This was our truck? There was no gate where there should have been one. All our stuff was back there, some of it inside boxes. I guess she was just praying to God it stayed put.

My door wouldn't open. She tried it from the inside, but it still wouldn't open. "Must be broke," she said. "Come around to my side." I went back around the truck, our truck, and crawled in through her door and over the seat.

"What you got there?" she asked me. "Nothing," I said. "I can see it's something," she said, "so stop trying to hide it." I showed it to her. "Cowboy Hall of Fame card," she said. "I see." "Can I keep it?" I asked. "Didn't I tell you not to go down there no more?" "I didn't," I said. "I was just giving him his records back." She shook her head. "Are you mad at me?" "You got too soft a heart, Bob," she said.

She shut the door and turned the engine over, but it wouldn't start. "Shit," she said. "What's wrong with it?" I asked. "Shit shit shit shit shit," she said. She kept trying and trying until she gave up. "This happens," she said. "Just means it's flooded. When this happens, just give it a minute, the man said." She took out a cigarette and punched in the lighter and waited. I looked out the window at the white paint and the brown dirt and all the food she threw at Lawton, still out there on the gravel. "Are we going somewhere?" I asked her. "What's it look like, Bob?" "Looks like we are," I said. "Where are we going?" "Not sure yet," she said. The lighter popped out, but she didn't light her cigarette; she just held the lighter in her hand and stared out the window. That was my mother, lost from the beginning of time. "Got any suggestions?" she asked.

More Abandon

(Or Whatever Happened to Joe Pope?)

They're leaving. An exodus. Out of the elevators, onto the street. Into the waning mild midwestern sunlight. Taking their first real breaths of the day. Thank God to be done with that. Lighting up cigarettes, loosening ties. Clustering at corners to await the light change. Joe Pope's window on sixty-two looks down on only a small tight angle of this manic outrush. The women returned to tennis shoes. The men without wives stopping in Burger Kings and Popeye's Fried Chickens for dubious meals laid out on laps during the express ride home. If they don't leave on the 6:12, they're stuck riding the milk train, making all the stops along the route—can't do that. Their evening hours are time-sensitive material made personal: they shimmy and jaywalk, juke and dart toward their destinations in a pathological state of hurry-up-and-get-home. Joe remains standing at his office window because, he tells himself, there is work to do. Looking down on an open courtyard, he watches people cut across angles of least resistance, heading toward buses, waiting taxis. Just beyond the courtyard, there's the entrance ramp to the Outer Drive, and the cars are lined up in tight formation to get on, all the city's to'd froing again the way they came. Light descends. It is the settling-in of dusk, the draining, abandoning psychology of dusk, and in a few minutes there will be an ebbing, a point of no return. But there is work to do, work to do, and that, he tells himself, is why he stays. It is nothing that can't wait until tomorrow, but he is incapable of breaking free.

Genevieve Latko-Devine has left. Benny Shassburger has left. Jim Jackers has gone for the night—Joe Pope's coworkers, his friends. Two doors down the hall, Shassburger keeps a pair of binoculars handy for the closer inspection of unsuspecting women on the rooftop pool of the Holiday Inn. The office without Shass is airless and quiet, stilled as it seldom is during day hours. But Shass has long cut out, and despite the neon Yuengling sign and collection of World Series caps on the walls, his office appears anonymous. Joe Pope stands hovering over the desk. He gets down on his haunches and rifles through the drawers. He wonders how creepy he looks. Finally he finds the binoculars under a stack of back issues of *Sports Illustrated,* and he takes to the hall again.

He goes to the office full of pigs. Oh, how fatiguing, he thinks, not for the first time—how vaguely oppressive. Pig calendars, pig posters ("It's been a trough day!"), stress relievers in the shape of pigs on top of her computer. Her name is Megan Korrigan and she loves pigs. Pig pencils, pink pig notepads, pig jokes taped to the door. Pigs hung from key chains pinned into corkboard. Her screen saver is a repeating pattern of dancing pigs, and the credenza is filled with pig figurines, piggy banks, stuffed-animal pigs, pigs made of glass and crystal, of eraser and plastic, porcelain Porky Pigs, and a Babe the Pig that talks when you pull its string. She keeps two copies of *Charlotte's Web* on her bookshelves, alongside marketing textbooks and binders full of branding guidelines, and hanging from her wall is a metal sign of a bibbed pig licking its lips, promoting the eating of itself by crying, "This way to the BBQ!" Why pigs? He walks past them and approaches the window. There is an orchid and three small rows of unbudded herbs in red clay pots. The need for green at work. Traps to catch the sun in. This he understands more clearly than pigs. He lifts the gray binoculars to his eyes.

This is the reason he's here: from Megan's northern office on the sixty-second floor, there is a clear view of the building opposite. He can see into fifteen floors of it, about twenty offices from left to right—roughly a total of three hundred windows set in the steely black glazing of skyscraper, easily penetrated by Shassburger's binoculars. The pattern of lit windows is switchboard random. Looking into the first window— what is he hoping to see? What relief will it bring? Must be something interesting going on in one of them.

More abandon. Light's on but no one's home. He eyes these interiors that resemble the interiors of the building he's in but strike him, because they're in a different building, as exotic, rife with sexual possibility. People in other offices have trysts on desks. It doesn't happen here—doesn't happen to him—but that it happens in that building over there seems inevitable. Plants along windowsills cascade over air-conditioning vents. Chairs are turned awry, screen savers churn. In one office, a small mobile, a red Calder reproduction, hangs from the soft tile ceiling, turning slowly in the central-air draft. There are only a handful of windows still lit, and those are empty. Finally, he finds a woman two floors down, a dozen windows over, sitting fortuitously near the window, turned to him and applying herself to paperwork. He trains and refocuses. Not his type. Hair like a fern, tight glossy curls. Bad blouse. He looks for some crack in it, revelation of body beneath. She's all sewn up. He keeps the glasses trained on the space between buttons, where the fabric sometimes poufs out, for the possibility of a glimpse. But no luck. And after a while it becomes no different from joining her at her paperwork. What relief there, what pleasure that?

He missed the window almost directly across from him, one floor down, from which light emanates. He quickly swings the binoculars around front and center, but no sooner does he do so than the light blinks off, a sunspot burning out. What, leaving? Why and where to? What plans have *you* made? He pictures a man. The man enters the hallway and heads toward the elevator bank. A handsome man, he's dressed in a gray suit with a starched white shirt mildly wrinkled after the crush and wrangle of a day, briefcase in hand, holding the suit coat over a shoulder with two fishhook fingers. Where does this image come from? Does it exist in real life, or only in the opening print ads of *GQ*? Well, *some*one just left, Joe saw the light go out, and just because he made it a man in a gray suit with a blue-and-tan striped tie and handsome features doesn't mean the man doesn't exist. He is just now taking the elevator to the lobby floor. He will climb into the back of a waiting cab. Where to, pal? Home? Meeting a woman in a bar? Now the cab is speeding away. The back of the man's head in the rearview window is disappearing toward the Inner Drive, and Joe's curiosity about the man's destination turns quickly into a kind of envy that has no object but the vague conviction that other people are happier and getting more out of life than he is. He is at work, still at work, no place to be but work, where there is work to do. Difficult to do work, though, when he wants to be out there with them. Where are they all going, those people in the backs of cabs?

He ventures into other offices with views onto other buildings. He takes the stairs to reception, on sixty-one, with its calla lilies and pitchers of cucumber-and-lime water. All the ice is melted, and the sofas are empty. He opens the glass door and enters another hallway. He goes into the first office on the right, which looks west. Ten minutes later, he leaves that office and takes the elevator to the sixty-sixth floor, passes the coffee bar, where he pauses for a few stale pretzels in a bowl. He continues past a cluster of cubicles and into a conference room, to a wall-length window. Standees of Tony the Tiger and the Pillsbury Doughboy lurk anthropomorphically in the corners. Here is where Shass goes to look down on the hotel's rooftop pool. Joe trains the binoculars out the window, but it is too dark now, and the pool is empty. No swimming after sundown. He walks to the north side of the building and enters another office — whose is this? Oh, what's-his-name — the guy collects snow globes. Go somewhere, bring back a snow globe, and he'll pay you for it. Appropriately harmless distraction, or a real passion? Joe can't imagine it either way. Turn it over and make it snow. There's some kind of pleasure in that? It sustains you? He walks up to the window. The sun's fully down now. Building tops reflect the black sky, roof spurs are blotted out, the construction crew working a half-finished skyscraper has gone home long ago. Stilled cranes angle in the air. Farther out is a blinking manic circuit board of light. Signal lights pulse faintly as airplanes circle holding patterns above O'Hare. Objectless longing again. Where do people go when they board planes? Who awaits them in the terminals, in purring SUVs, in warm beds across the hushed and longing land? He is office-locked, deskbound, and how did that happen? He trains the binoculars down on the building across the way and into an angle of windows where no human presence offers itself again.

Joe, Joseph — go home, for God's sake, he can hear someone telling him. His father: "Get your butt home, boy. Call someone. Make plans. Enjoy your youth. It only comes around once."

But who could he call that doesn't work here? Who would it be that he won't see tomorrow?

He window-shops like this till late in the evening. Part of the night he gives over to the contemplation of why his colleagues put such things on their walls. What it means to be the person who hangs up autographed eight-by-tens, African masks. There is one office — Janine Gorjanc's office — filled with pictures of her murdered child. Everyone knows the story. The child was taken from an open window. The body wasn't found for months. And only many months after that did Janine return to work, now bearing pictures of the dead girl. Everyone avoids the office like the plague. Several of the frames are meant for a flat surface, so across the desk and bookshelves, and the credenza along the back wall, and on top of her filing cabinet, any number of overlapping eight-by-tens proliferate at cross-purposes. Others hang from the wall — Jessica straight

on, quarter profile floating in white cloud; Jessica in T-ball out-
fit; Jessica on her father's knee. Janine's office is among the
most mournful things Joe has ever seen, as when a soldier dies
and a shrine appears. The first time he entered it and saw the
sheer quantity of photos, he found himself reluctant to move.
It was like finding the walls covered in bats. There was a fluttering, and a hum in the air, and he didn't want to move too
quick lest they all fly up and start screaming.

Without his knowing it, the lobby guards change shifts. So
do the security men monitoring the television banks. Hispanic
women in uniforms emerge from the elevator, trundling supply
carts and industrial vacuums. This is the other side of things,
the time of lockdown and cleanup, when the tenders of the
building replace its daytime occupiers in order to keep the occupiers from noticing the things to which they tend. One of
the vacuumers, with the full lips and sad oval eyes of a dispossessed princess, sees Joe as she pushes her cart down a hallway.
He emerges from an office holding binoculars, walks across the
hallway and enters another office. He doesn't see her. Then he
wanders out of the second office just as quickly and begins to
walk toward her. They are both startled—she that he is coming toward her, and he that she is present at all. He's wearing a
navy-blue button-down and belted pleated slacks, a shiny pair
of black oxfords. He commands a presence in this space, she
thinks, more vital in the hierarchy than her own, and she averts
her eyes. She is beautiful, he thinks, and must be wondering
why he is still here long after he should have gone home, and
he averts his eyes. They pass each other by.

An hour later, he is sitting in Jim Jackers's office in a chair
of remarkable comfort, an ergonomic triumph, holding Jim's

phone in contemplation. Not to his ear but in the cradle of his shoulder, so that he can hear the faint hum of the dial tone. He likes Jim's office better than his own. Shaped the same. The same ceiling-tile count. But somehow Jim has made his more anonymous—absolutely nothing here that couldn't be packed away within minutes. He looks around for even a single personal item. People must wonder about Jim more than they do about him. Is that what it means to put stuff on your walls—that people no longer feel a need to wonder about you? Sports, old movies, pigs—doesn't matter, so long as you take an interest in something. He reaches out and renews the dial tone. Well, should he call?

Oh, what the hell. He dials, knowing the phone will ring, ring, ring, until it goes to voicemail. Not your average voicemail. That voice. Tone of hope, pitch of happiness. If the small of a woman's back could sing. What's she saying? "Hello, you've reached Genevieve Latko-Devine at the Brand Investment Group. I'm away from my desk at the moment, but if you'll leave—" This is normally as far as he gets. He calls to hear her voice, not to leave his message. He cups the phone in his hand. He shifts in the chair. He should hang up and call back, play the message again. There are nights, make of them what you will, when he repeats the exercise beyond the reasonable. Sometimes calling from his apartment, midnight, two in the morning. Four, five beers roiling in his stomach, television blaring mutely, alarm set for six. He feels moderately less unhealthy now calling from Jim's office. Its cold officeness gives the enterprise a veneer of legitimacy, as if he might be reminding her of a meeting tomorrow morning or changes that need inputting. Is he going to hang up now or what?

"...encountering an emergency, please press one now, and you will be directed to—" He hangs on nervously, anguished by the possibility of saying something into the machine without really knowing what that might be, of having nothing to say but wanting to say something anyway. He's afraid of himself. Time is never so real—never so forcefully marching on—as when he hears her voice unfurling scripted instructions to leave a message and, at the end of it, after the beep, he's forced to confront himself. That unprescribed longing, the inarticulate, memorialized, permanent confession that every time, somehow, he just restrains himself from issuing into that perfect hostage, the telephone.

Beep—

"Hey, Eve—"

Do two little words give him away? Bittersweet that she might know his voice so well. But could he hang up now and deny it tomorrow?

"—this is, uh—"

Not if he says his name...

"—it's Joe."

He pauses. What the Jesus God almighty do I think I'm doing?

"It's about, uh—"

Do not be honest about the time.

"—eight thirty, nine thirty, something like that, I'm still at the, I'm still at the office, if you can believe it, just trying to, uh, just finishing—getting a lot of stuff that's been piling up lately, like, well, you know, you know how...And I was looking over your, uh, your—the ads you did for the hardware convention? The banner ads. And I thought, I should call, because those are really, the images are really beautiful. Hard to believe we're selling hammers. We should be selling, I don't know what. They're that good. What they reminded me of was, they reminded me so much of those screen prints we saw at the Contemporary. Remember? We were there for lunch, I think, like, when was that, six months ago? I forget the woman's name. But when I saw these, I thought of those screen prints. You'll have to remind me of her name. Ha, ha, am I just blabbering into your machine?"

Here begins a long pause. He should cut his losses and hang up. But something strange happens as the pause expands. He comes to realize that it might be possible to separate what he's now saying into the phone from the anxiety he feels at the prospect of her listening to it in the morning. Separating the message he's leaving from the message she'll play back, separating them into two distinct realities—one that he commands and sanctions and is all about him, the other vaguer, involving her (and something he doesn't have to think about just yet). It takes the pressure off momentarily. Relax. Talk. What's the big deal? They're friends. He's just talking to an old friend here, and he settles back into Jim Jackers's chair.

"Yeah," he says, "I guess I am just blabbering into your machine. Can't you tell? Are you still there? Still listening?" Another pause. "What do I want to say?" A third pause. "I did call for a reason, believe it or not. There were any number of people I could have called, but you were the first one I thought of when I thought to call someone. And I know that it's not really talking when you leave a message, that's not really talking, but I'd feel weird calling you at home right now, obviously. You might be sleeping, or your husband might pick up. It's really more like ten fifteen, to be honest. Ten thirty. Maybe I should feel even weirder leaving a message. It's a little, I don't know, a little one sided...well, yeah, it's just so one sided. But I really, I wanted to, uh, to say how lately I've been feeling...What I want to say is how great you are—" Oh, Jesus. *Great?* Really? "—how great I think you are, and that we've worked together for, how long, like, three years now, and in that time I've—"

"If you're satisfied with your message, please press one now. To listen to your message, please press two. To rerecord your message, please press three."

Well, he thinks, it all works out in the end. Joe Pope doesn't have to send his train wreck of a message after all. Press three and it's all erased. The quivering, that sped-up heart and stomach full of jumble—all false alarms in the end. Even his minor triumph—his refusal to be cowed by the indelible recordedness of the things he was saying, and by his future accountability to them—can be rendered moot now by the press of a button. He should be grateful. So why is his finger poised above the one button? Why is there part of him that *wants* to send it?

He leaves her a total of five messages. He's cut off from each one after three minutes. When the recorded voice interrupts him to give him options, he presses one every time. Fifteen minutes of message, in which he tells her everything. How he loves her. How she is the reason he gets up in the morning and is eager to return to work. How her presence beside him in meetings, that arbitrary arrangement, means everything to him. How unmoored he feels lately, how rudderless. How lunch with her gives him some sense of purpose, and how quickly lost he becomes after five o'clock, when she leaves for home. He knows she can't love him back. The irrefutability of it has been made clear by the fact that she is pregnant. And now he fears losing her because the baby is due soon. He attacks himself for this selfishness and says into the phone that he could not be happier for her, honest. And that leads him into darker, more vulnerable territory. Why does her life cast a shadow over his own? Why does her happiness, hers and her husband's, follow him everywhere he goes, quietly qualifying the things that might normally bring him delight? Walking his dog on a Sunday afternoon—why does this simple pleasure turn into something irredeemably sad? Why does a cab ride through the city without her make him an empty and unrealized dreamer? And since when, and by what right, has he hitched his happiness to hers and forsaken the power to be the source of his own contentedness?

His relief when he finally hangs up the phone is immense. How long he has wanted to tell her these things. Three long years of days. Consider the discipline it takes. Consider the agony of a single weekend, when she flees the space in which he loves her for her real and substantial life—the one she shares with someone else—leaving him with the pathetic desire for the weekend to speed by so that *his* real and substantial life can begin again. Fool! What depths of despair are you trawling when your happiness hinges upon work—the meetings you both attend, projects you share, the gossip she lets you in on? Is that why you're still here, when there is all that life to be had out there, beyond the office? Joe Pope had tried to tell himself he was here to do work. But there is nothing that can't wait until tomorrow. He is here because he feels closer to Genevieve at the office than he does at home.

He *had* to tell her, didn't he? Had to unburden. Otherwise the years would continue to pass, and he would end up, what? A slight and regretful old man. Feel good about yourself, then, Joe. It was long overdue! Husband, baby—what does any of that matter? For Joe Pope, they are beside the point. He's not even sure the torch he carries concerns *her* anymore. It's a fixation now, an obsession. His days are hell, his nights are worse, something had to give.

So why does he feel juuuuust a little anxious? Well, it's not easy to confess love, not to anyone, not even to an immense heart like Genevieve's, that boundless heart, that ever-widening and sympathetic heart. What power a confession of love confers upon the beloved, what opportunity for a flattening. But look at what's been gained. There's reclamation. There's taking charge of his life. And the unburdening—hey, the relief of the unburdening can't be underestimated. And that *was* the whole point, was it not, to unburden? Because what could he hope to gain by telling her of his love when she has a husband, and a baby on the way? Yes, the unburdening was all.

Brian Ford, manic media buyer and martini drinker, keeps a pack of emergency smokes in a top desk drawer. Joe heads down to sixty-five and teases a bent pipe of a cigarette from Ford's pack and returns by hallway and elevator to Megan Korrigan's office, to smoke among the BBQ pigs. He lies down on the carpeted floor of Megan's office and, smoking in defiance of building and city ordinances, ashes into the orchid he's dragged down there with him. Despite a kindling anxiety, he feels good. Laughing the spontaneous, mysteriously prompted, rock-bottom laughter of the recently shriven, he stabs out the cigarette in the orchid's vase and rests for a moment, a blue forearm thrown over his eyes. Light here never goes out completely. Always a little hallway light. Stay the night and no true rest will be had. But at a point when he's dazed enough not to notice the soft trundling of a supply cart down the hallway, the cleaning woman, the dispossessed princess, catches a glimpse of what might be a heel, two heels, a pair of legs — is that a person? Is someone asleep on the floor in there? He missed the sound of her, but the momentary heat of her stare is enough to make him remove his forearm. He sees a doorway figure. He sits up just as she moves on, and both of them shiver uneasily over the next moment or two, her down the hall, him on the office floor, in the recognition of catching and being caught doing something human.

There's something human, too, suddenly, about all these pigs. He looks around him. He's not sure he's seen it before just now. The sheer number of them on display has made it impossible to pay attention to any particular one. It's their combined effect that dominates. But from where he sits on the floor, he begins to make out individual pig expressions: ruddy cheeks, heads half-cocked, drowsy brows at half-mast. They sit like babies in a Michelin commercial. They stand on tip-hooves in a balletic twirl. He's going from pig to pig when the anxiety he's been trying to suppress explodes inside him: he has just left fifteen minutes of unchecked confession on Genevieve's voicemail! Holy shit! And what was the purpose again? Can't locate it! Was it, uh…something about unburdening? He's not remembering clearly. It was something, something prompted him only a half hour ago, when it all seemed so appropriate…yes, to unburden. But was that it? Or was there something more? Uh, yeah, there was, and now he can see it clearly. He allowed himself to hope. That despite the husband and the baby-to-be, she might play back those messages, run down to his office, and confess that she harbors feelings for him.

Oh, fool! Delusional fool! He has to find a way to erase them!

But first, he needs to do something with the pigs. It's worse for them here than a life on the farm. At least there they can oink around, nose each other's asses, roll over in the warm muck. Here they look infinitely more penned in. They never leave. They never move. They're ignored, undusted, calling out. They should prefer the slaughterhouse.

He returns from Marnie Telpner's office with shopping bags, into which he begins to carefully place one pig after the other, thinking, Feel good about yourself. It's liberating. Like these pigs here. It had to be done. For your own sake, if not for hers. Joe is spinning himself the other way again, back to the feel-good story. He tells himself, It had to be done, right? To unburden. It had nothing to do with hope. How Genevieve responds to the information doesn't even matter. Keep that in mind. It's beside the point. Hope is beside the point. What's important is, what's important...What exactly, Joe, do you plan on doing with all those pigs?

He removes the last of them—the wall calendar, the BBQ sign—and carries them down the hall.

Idiot! He spins himself back just as quickly. Two times an idiot! Once in recording the message and once in sending it! And how do you think she's going to respond, when he's just revealed himself to be a lonely, anguished, lovesick, delusional fool? Confessing defeats his very purpose. He wants her to admit that she, too, has feelings for him, but how could Genevieve love a fool?

He takes the bag full of pigs and enters Janine Gorjanc's office. When Janine returned after her child's funeral, she cried during input meetings. Once she cried walking into the men's room without realizing her mistake. She encouraged everyone who came into her office to read the newspaper clippings she kept in an album and to pick up the frames on her desk and look into the blue eyes of the dead girl. Months have passed since then when Joe takes one of the frames in his hands—it is now as dusty as Megan's pigs. He collects all the frames from the desk and the credenza and those hanging on the wall and puts them in a corner. Everyone has grown so familiar with the girl's tragedy that they don't see her face anymore. Not even her mother, who on some days can be very busy. With nervous energy he replaces the frames with Megan's figurines. Pigs begin to populate across wood grains, over disheveled papers, on the dusty top of Janine's clock radio. He hangs pig key chains from frame hooks, the calendar and BBQ sign from nails that once supported pictures of the girl. The pigs appear refreshed in their new setting, ridiculous smiles renewed. Then he packs the frames into the shopping bag and carries them down the hall. He sets them up across all the pig-free surfaces of Megan's desk, pointing the lost child's smiling face into the hall, so that everyone will have no choice but to notice her again, in the morning, as they walk by.

Around one now. He ends up in Genevieve's office, a floor below his own and a better place to be. It's carefully decorated with merchandise from art museum gift shops—a clock that bobs on a stem, miniature Eames chairs on the windowsill. On the wall behind the desk is a Rothko reproduction in a red plastic frame. And on her desk are photographs of her adoring husband. The message light on her phone beats a steady red pulse. Might it give out by morning? No more likely than his own sturdy heart. He picks up the receiver and presses the message light. The same conspiring female voice that prompted him to press one now instructs him to input Genevieve's PIN. He tries her birthday. He tries her address. He tries 1234. He spends a good half hour going through various combinations. In a moment of truly lush preposterousness, he tries his own name plus zero. Then his own name plus one, plus two, et cetera. Eventually he resigns himself to not knowing what four digits are closest to her heart.

Maybe it's the phone. Are messages stored in the phone, or in the wires, the connections, some central processing hub? What *is* a message? What if he were to disconnect the cord and replace it with a different phone—say, his own? He could easily switch it with one from a closer office, but her receiver, he's noticed, emits a musky variation on her shampoo, something he'd like to have for himself. So he carries it up to his office and returns down the stairs with his phone in hand. He has the sudden feeling of being watched. That cleaning lady! He turns his head quickly but finds only that pattern of diminishing office doors and, at hallway's end, the blank expression of a door to an office that belongs to someone long gone home.

When the switcheroo fails to stop her message light from blinking, he considers the wholesale theft of Genevieve's phone. But Kathy the office manager would quickly find her a new one, and when Genevieve got around to finally checking her messages, who would she suspect had stolen the old one?

Teddy Reiser keeps a toolbox under his desk in the event something should go wrong during a photo shoot. Joe takes a Phillips-head from Teddy's office and returns to Genevieve's, where, with the door closed, he opens the silver wall plate supporting the phone cord. With a pair of dull scissors, he works his way through many thin, multicolored wires. The phone goes dead, thank God. But he doesn't stop there. Only cutting the phone lines will look suspicious. People will wonder why they were cut, and if ever the messages surface— Wait, he thinks: won't recorded messages survive cut phone lines? . . . Oh, God!—they will know it was him. But will they know it, would they even ever suspect it, if there was more than cut phone lines?

And so, without much thought or deliberation, his crimes snowball. He gathers up all her personal things, including the pictures of her husband and the Rothko reproduction, and places them, for the time being, in the corner, while he carefully vandalizes her office. Doesn't want to do any actual damage, though, so with the deliberateness of an artist he lays the phone on the ground in a way that suggests tossed-off violence. He does the same with the documents on her desk. He unshelves the books, eases the bookshelves down onto the floor, and places everything at a rakish angle. Standing on her chair, he pulls on the latticework of metal that holds the ceiling tiles together. The ceiling buckles. A few of the tiles he removes, setting them down where they were likely to fall anyway. He turns over the chair and the computer monitor. Then he retrieves her undamaged belongings and places them, including the picture of her husband, gently upon the ground, between gaps of destruction. The last thing he does is rehang her reproductions.

Leaving, he shuts the light off. An odd scruple. But it's not *the* world that needs destroying, just his world. And shutting off the light just seems the right thing to do.

They're coming back. To the footstep, the wheel turn, returning to their stations from the day before. The El cars are crammed, each a tinderbox of body heat and morning breath, and there's stop-and-go traffic on the highways. Everyone converging on the city's center of gravity: the skyline in the distance. There is every suggestion of renewal in the sun's slow predominating, as it warns them of another long day ahead. The early-morning shine begins to slake the buildings' black-metal thirst for heat. They deboard from trains and subways, hundreds of them, from buses and taxis, gaining the street from the platform stairs. Shouldering backpacks, pulling luggage carts over the curbs and potholes, they become vaguely aware of last night's storm by skirting around pools of opalescent rainwater. Otherwise, not much thought in the head at this hour. In the last few blocks, their paths present inefficiencies that must be indulged: they go afield for lattes, fruit cups, fat-free muffins, packs of cigarettes, aspirins to cut the morning dread. Oh, don't want to go back there. Have to go back there. Here we all are again, happy to be back.

Joe Pope the dependable one wakes in Sonya Hutton's office, sharing her upholstered couch with Benny's binoculars and a racquetball racket. There's an electric guitar at his feet. Sonya is at her desk early this morning, eating breakfast from a black container and listening to NPR on an antique Bakelite radio. He feels he is waking into a dream, a soft-lit and underwater world of cold sunshine, broadcast voices, and cooked eggs.

Sonya is uncomfortably near—not much room between him, on the sofa, and her, at the desk. She is looking right at him, tree-stump calf and combat boot elevated to desk level, egg trough in one hand and plastic fork in the other. "Comfortable?" she inquires.

"Not really," Joe replies, rising to sitting position. A lick of hair on the left side stands straight up like a wall of tiny feathers. "I'm in your office, am I?"

"Mi casa es su casa," she says. "Sofa's company issued, anyway, and the smell will go away. What's with the guitar?"

Joe has to think. It was that tricky, anxious hour between the decision to sleep and sleep itself when he took it from Gary Need's office. Bad choice of bedmate, an electric guitar, both cumbersome and cold. The racket belongs to Trish Miller.

After destroying Genevieve's office, he found himself down at Trish's, where he discovered a gym bag and racquetballs. He thought he'd work off some nervous energy, keyed into the gym, and batted the ball around barefoot until a Rorschach-like stain blossomed down the front of Trish's snug University of Wisconsin T-shirt. He found that in the gym bag, too. He looks down. He's still in it.

"What time is it?" he asks.

Sonya, peering up into a wall-mounted Hamm's beer light box and clock display, where a fountain of white water flows eternally into a crystal stream behind the black hands of time itself, currently moving the morning forward, and Joe toward a reckoning with last night—Sonya squints and admits to not having her glasses. Eight thirty, she guesses. "Were you here all night?"

He was, but that's all over with now. Time now to start the

day. And in the daylight this is no place for indulging the inefficiencies of human need. Joe Pope isn't a worker bee, but nor is he quite the boss here, either. As dreaded middle management, he's tasked with more than most around here and is damned dependable. Ordinarily at this hour, you'd find him arriving, well rested and squeaky clean, with bagel bag in hand, left pant leg pinned back for the bike ride in, as deadlines and priorities started to percolate through his caffeinated mind. Not so now. Joe took leave of his senses last night, and in the light of day, he's wondering what he should do about that.

To be honest, they probably won't press charges. Fire him, sure, and require that he pay for the damages—but arrest him? He's Joe Pope. He's beloved around here.

"I did it," he says.

"Did what?"

As if on cue, there's a sudden commotion, that call to gather and witness some strange happening in an otherwise staid workplace.

"What did you do, Joe?" she asks.

He leans back on the sofa, and air breathes out of the cushion through a cigarette burn. "First, I looked out the windows with Shassburger's binoculars. He has a good pair of binoculars. I did that for about three hours. I was looking for something interesting."

"Find anything?"

"Nothing. So then I smoked one of Brian Ford's cigarettes."

"I've done that."

"And then I took all of Megan's pigs out of her office, and I switched them with all the pictures in Janine's office."

"Switched them?"

"Right. I took the pigs in Megan's office, and I brought them down to Janine's office, and then I took all the pictures of Jessica that Janine has in her office, and I brought them down to Megan's office. So now the pigs are in Janine's and Jessica is in Megan's."

Sonya lets her combat boot fall to the floor. "You serious?" Between "you" and "serious," a yellow speck of egg flies from her mouth and lands somewhere between her and Joe. They acknowledge it unspokenly.

"How does that strike you?" he asks.

"So I could go up there right now and see all the pigs in Janine's office."

"Uh-huh."

"And all the pictures of the dead girl in Megan's office."

"Yep."

Sonya sets the plastic container of eggs on her desk and picks up her coffee. Her underwear is bunched under her cut-off fatigues, and she wiggles to free it. "This I got to see."

"Start in Genevieve's office," he says. "I'm responsible for that, too."

She leaves him on the sofa. His back aches and his head aches and the smell of eggs makes him want to flee the building. Run, never to return. But he doesn't. This is just who he is in the a.m. A man responsible for things.

He stands and stretches—necessary to start the day off right. Then he returns the guitar to the stand in Gary's office. In Trish's office, he discovers his blue button-down, which he draped last night across Trish's chair. He makes the switch. The size medium Wisconsin tee is stretched out and not nearly as clean as it was when he found it. But it's back in

Trish's gym bag now and, frankly, low on the scale of his concerns.

In the bathroom on sixty, he tries to work down sleep's cowlick like a cat, but it's a stubborn little fucker, and he gives up. The hallways are starting to crackle with the day's coping banter. He takes a seat behind his desk, swipes the screen saver away with his mouse, and answers a few final emails. Then he sits back in the swivel chair, spins around to face the sun in the window, and waits.

Fragments

Here's a question I've always wanted to ask. When you're up there, are there coordinates you have to follow, or are you free to go anywhere you like?"

"Depends on where in the city you are. If you come near any of the airports, obviously —"

"Oh, sure."

"Which you need clearance to do, anyway."

"I'm just talking about, like, say you're over Midtown."

"I don't do Midtown. There's another guy does Midtown."

"I'm saying, what if you just happened to find yourself there?"

"Let me tell you," the second man said, laughing. "You never just find yourself inside a chopper in Midtown."

He stopped eavesdropping on them when the call from Katy came in. He picked up, hoping that her deadline had been pushed back, that she'd changed her mind, that she'd be joining him after all.

"Hey," he answered.

No reply. Static. A physical thing, a trail of it. Static heading somewhere, progressing down a hallway.

"Katy?" he said.

Static crumpling and ironing itself out. A quick vacuum silence, then more jostle. "Katy," he said again. "Helloooo." He stepped out of the bar, knowing by then that his wife hadn't intended to call him. "Kaaa-teee!" he sang. Static shifting, churning, then lifting suddenly. He hollered to be heard. "Yoo-hoo, Katy!"

"... no, he thinks I'm..."

More static.

"... just wish... could spend the night..."

Then a man's voice. "... too bad you live... have an extra hour..."

More static. He plugged his other ear and listened intently. The words were torn before they reached him, irrecoverable. He was no longer saying her name, just listening.

"... dinner, but if you're not..."

"... hungry all right, but not for..."

He listened for who knows how long. Only fragments came through. Amplified, then muted. He strained to identify the man's voice. It was low and familiar. Long periods of static gave way to discrete words, occasional phrases.

He stood in the cold trying to interpret them. By then, he knew his life was over.

He hung up, then called her back almost immediately. It went straight to voicemail. It went to voicemail a second time. Finally, it rang, but rang and rang.

He went back inside the bar. The indiscriminate noise of the other patrons registered as a murmur. He didn't take a seat but hovered over his drink, staring at it without touching it. He'd known. That was the thing. Somehow he'd known.

When Katy came in that night, it was late and he was asleep. And she was gone again long before he woke. That was how it was most nights, now that the case was going to trial.

He showered and had coffee. He took his time leaving the apartment. He drifted through the rooms, looking at their many things. What a pain in the ass it would be to sort through it all.

Out on the street, he fell in step with a girl on the phone. "No, he already graduated from law school," she said. "He's getting his master's degree in real estate from NYU."

There was a long pause. "A master's degree in . . . I think real estate. Why are you laughing?"

There was another pause. "Why would he lie about something so— Stop laughing!"

The subway was packed. The black kid said to his friend, "The scope was fat. She was at it for like an hour."

"How many shots?" his friend asked.

One of the seated women peered over.

"Who cares when it's dead?" the first kid said.

On his lunch hour, he left the office and walked around. He went to Central Park and back, a full mile. He watched the ground but remained oblivious of the pennies, the gum stamps, the pigeons twitching in the cold. For long passages, nothing penetrated the roar in his head.

He stood at the crosswalk.

"So we're like a fund of funds, because we take a stake,

but we can't, you know, we have, what, a ten, maybe twenty percent—"

"Right," the other guy said.

"Anyway, he's an asshole, but he makes money."

"Best kind of asshole."

He passed two women without coats smoking outside a building.

"Seriously, girl," the one said.

"I know, I know—but can I just tell you what he does?"

The second woman drew closer and whispered into the ear of her companion, who gasped. "Get out!" she cried.

He slogged through the day. After work he went to the gym. He sat down in the locker room and was removing his shoes as two guys he knew by sight were on their way out.

"But not female masturbation, just male masturbation."

"So you fap yourself?"

"But just dudes. The word for female's, like...no, I don't remember it."

He couldn't bring himself to undress, so he sat there. Three young guys came in, smelling of recently smoked cigarettes, and waited for the one to change out of his street clothes. "But what are you going to eat at a buffet?" the first guy asked. "I mean, are you going to eat the sushi, or are you going to go straight for the fucking...you know, the fucking—"

"Not the fucking sushi."

"I'll tell you why she wants to go there."

"Yeah, did she lose weight?"

"Thirty pounds."

"Yeah, she looks good."

"Why do you think we're...?"

The first guy quickly punched his fist in and out.

He abandoned the smelly clothes in his gym bag, the gym bag itself, everything, and left the locker room.

"Goodbye," the woman at the front desk said to him on his way out. "Have a good night."

He ate at a diner uptown, far from the apartment. He sat alone, listening to the conversation going on in the booth behind him.

"Like, he found a day job that makes him happy," the hipster said. "He genuinely likes coffee. Where it's from, what the blend is, shit like that."

The Asian girl on the far side said something he couldn't hear.

"Because I don't want to go back to Lafayette. Or Tulsa."

That night, Katy came home later than usual. He was up but feigned sleep. With the lights off, she tiptoed into the bedroom, making no effort to wake him. He wanted her to. He wanted her to say something, anything, but she slid in lightly and was asleep in no time. What hurt more—her peaceful sleep, or the silence that preceded it? He got up and walked to the couch. It was late when he woke. She was gone, of course.

On the street, the free a.m. newspaper was shouting about the coming blizzard. The flakes were just starting to whiten shoulders, driving in a pattern not always easy to make sense of.

"Excuse me," he cried out on the platform. "Excuse me!"

The man ahead of him had dropped a glove.

"Oh, thanks," the man said.

"You're welcome."

"I do that all the time," the man said, turning away from him, back to his companion.

"Anyway, I don't know if he bought it or not," his companion continued.

"Why would a scarf cost fifteen hundred dollars?"

"Why would he buy it? That's the question."

They all climbed up the subway stairs together. The man was still happy to have his gloves. "I swear I lose these things all the time," he said, swatting the glove on his leg as he walked. "I've probably lost a hundred pairs."

On his lunch hour, another walk. This time, he made it down to Union Square. The sky was a sheet of tin hanging low. He walked north, past Meatball Obsession. "Home of the Original Meatball in a Cup." He passed Sol Moscot Opticians and all the chains along Sixth. He passed a former church, now Heavenly Laser and Beauty Lounge.

"Scrubs!" the first man cried. "Can you imagine needing scrubs?"

"Hey, with that one there's nothing more important than making sure everything's sterile."

The first man howled with laughter.

Another long afternoon at work, during which there was no call or email from his wife. On his way home, in the corridors of the subway, he overheard the woman tell the man to slow down. "Where we sitting at?" the woman asked. They were far from any bench and far from the platform. The man turned.

"Why I'm sitting? Where?"

"You ain't sitting?"

"Why I'm sitting for? Sitting for what?"

"I'm just saying."

"I'm not sitting nowhere. I'm trying to get to the train. What I'm sitting for?"

Again he lay in bed, waiting for her, but it was one, two in the morning and impossible to stay awake. When he woke in the dark, she was deadweight beside him, facing away, still dressed in her work clothes. He wondered what to do. Should he wake her? Sooner or later, something had to be done.

The next morning, he stopped for a bagel. The espresso machines were crying bloody murder. The man in line behind him said, "Hey, it was her idea...I sleep just fine, thank you...That's not for me to worry about, that's the husband's deal. And don't tell me you'd have done anything different..."

When he glanced back, he discovered that the man wasn't on a cell phone but was talking to an old woman who could barely raise her voice above a whisper.

Back on the street, he realized he wasn't hungry and threw the bagel away. He walked to work, all thirty-eight blocks.

The blizzard had been canceled. Only a light dusting had fallen after all. Still, it was slippery, and he felt out of control with every step.

"I need to place an order," the man at the corner said. "Forsythe. Newark. Forty-two hundred gallons of crude."

He went into Brooklyn on his lunch hour, all the way to Coney Island on the train. It was cold on the boardwalk. The sky was overcast, clotted with bruised clouds. They turned the nearer distances blue. He didn't go back in to work but called in sick.

"I was under the illusion that if I just kept moving from one to the other, I'd never die."

"That just makes it easier for death to sneak up on you," the second man said.

Guys were working on the track. They wore reflector vests and hard hats. One of them said, "You got the numbers written down? Clear it out. Clear it out—we'll go to the other side. Was there a roll? Never mind, we'll just go to the other side."

At home, he looked away from their things and out the window, at the city, and saw almost nothing: fading light, a growing density, shadows walking below. That was the night she didn't come home.

The blizzard was back on. The snow fell in an unrelieved trance. It slanted across every street-lamp glow. In the morning, there was nothing, only white. The flakes came hissing to the ground, disappearing like ash. People walked like they were on the moon.

He stopped for coffee. Everyone was talking about the blizzard.

"No cab nowhere. I'm looking at two o'clock in the morning. By then, I swear to God, I'm going out of my mind."

"How is he now?"

"Not good. Maybe...I don't know, Cheryl, maybe I should have just put him down last week."

The second counter girl said, "Hello, can I take your order?"

He didn't go in to work that day. His breath in his ears, the scraping of a shovel in the distance, the crunch of every cumbered step—these were the only sounds, and they filled the silence of the snowbound world. The man with the sparking shovel whistled a tune as he passed.

Then the taxis started to move. The snow got stamped down. At the corners, the slush churned.

When night fell, he stopped at a bodega near the apartment, looking for something to eat.

The man said, "They taking them?"

"Over my dead body they taking them. Them my two little girls, man."

When they realized he was there, they clammed up. He went home and ate what he'd bought and then he went to the bar.

"Everybody wants him," the man nearest him said. "Everybody."

"B.L.A.?"

"Everybody."

"That's hard to believe."

"If I could kill myself without dying, if I could kill myself and instead of dying he died, I'd do it in a heartbeat."

"Wouldn't that be murder?"

On his way home, the woman threw her arms down, out of the man's grasp. "No!" she cried. "It is not that easy! It is not that easy!"

"Shh, shh, shh."

"Hands off me!"

He went around them a little wide, then stopped and looked back. The man had turned her and lifted her off the ground while she struggled to free herself, legs kicking. He was prepared to step in if the man went any further, but he let go, and the woman dropped to the ground. She hit him with both fists over and over, blows he took laughing.

"Fucking suck it, Dom!" she cried, and walked off.

The man kicked a garbage bin, and the sound echoed. The

man turned almost immediately and shouted at him. "What the fuck are you looking at?"

He moved on.

He kept the lights off in the apartment. He was sitting on the sofa, snow melting at his feet, when the phone rang.

"Hello?"

"Hey!" she said. "So, I'm going to be late again tonight."

He didn't say anything.

"Cooke wants all the new discovery done by Monday morning. So...I don't know, around midnight, maybe?"

"How come you didn't come home last night?"

"No, no—not the McKinley docs. The Byrne docs, the Byrne docs!"

"Katy?"

"Sorry," she said. "Idiots."

"Did you hear me?"

"What did you say?"

"You didn't come home last night."

"I know. This case. It's driving everyone crazy."

He remained silent.

"Hello?" she said.

He hung up. He leaned over and turned on the light.

He went around turning on all the lights. They had a lot of stuff. There were books and magazines and travel guides and framed prints on the wall. There were lamps and stockpots and beds. There were stacks of CDs and milk crates of shoes and the bikes they rode in the summer.

There were things that were "his" and things that were "hers," a distinction from long ago that now reasserted itself with cruel haste. Every "her" thing was a reminder. She was "her" now, just that, no longer Katy, no longer his wife. He would call her "her" for the rest of his life.

He walked through the apartment. He'd done this two nights in a row. He was sick of doing it. Everything that was "hers" hurt one way. Things that were "theirs" hurt differently. The last thing he wanted was to have to divide it all up. He wanted things to go back to the way they had been, whole, undifferentiated. But there was no going back. It was broken. Everything mocked him and made him sad.

He took out his phone, intending to call someone, one of his friends. He could no longer keep it to himself. But he put the phone away, as he had before. He couldn't face it. And yet he needed to talk.

He went to the window. He looked down on the people passing below. Except for a patch in front of the church, most of the sidewalk on both sides of the street had been cleared of snow, and people moved freely. To his surprise, he called out. "Hey," he said. It wasn't loud enough. "Hey!" The man looked up without slowing down but couldn't locate him. He refrained from calling out a third time, and the man moved on. He hadn't anticipated calling out at all.

A minute later, a woman walking her dog came down the street. "Hey!" he said to her. She looked directly up at him. Well? she and the dog seemed to be asking. "Sorry," he said, and closed the window.

A few minutes later, he was back, head leaning over the ledge. He called out to a man and a woman. This time, he said, "Hey, you! Yeah, you! Stop, will you? Just for a sec?" The couple went quiet but continued walking. "I have something to

tell you!" he continued. The man stopped and said, "Is everything okay?" He wanted to be honest with the man. "No," he
said. "Nothing is okay."

He climbed up and crouched in the open window, steadying
the tips of his shoes and most of his weight on the jutting
brick. "My life's over," he said. The man took a step in his direction and removed his hands from his pockets.

"What are you doing up there?" After a while, the man said,
"It's dangerous up there."

Eventually, he stepped back inside.

"What the hell?" the man said as they resumed walking.

"Some kind of joke?" his companion replied.

He was back at the window a few minutes later. Now he
said, "My wife's having an affair." The man he addressed was
trying to make it over the icy patch in front of the church. The
affair was embarrassing to admit out loud, but he wanted to
stop the man, make him understand. After clearing the ice, the
man slowed and raised his head to the window. "Did you hear
me?" he hollered. "My wife's having an affair!" It was easier to
say the second time. "Good for you," the man said, and kept
moving.

A minute later, he said, "Hey!" and that man didn't stop,
but the next one did. "My wife's having an affair!" he said.
"Yeah?" the man said. He was almost directly below him and
really had to crane his neck. "What are you going to do to her?"
the man asked. He didn't like the way the man was just standing there looking up at him, smiling. He'd picked the wrong
man. "You gonna kill her?" the man asked. He stayed away
from the window until the man was gone.

The next man who stopped listened for a while. He told

him about his long nights and drifting days. Then he said, "Hey, you want something of hers?" The man seemed confused. "Come up, take something of hers. Take whatever you want."

"No, thanks," the man said. He started to move on. "But good luck to you."

"Hey!" he cried out to the next guy. "You want something from up here?" Without stopping, the man said, "Huh?" "Come up! Come up, take something." To his surprise, the man stopped. "I'm serious, come up. I'll buzz you up."

"What for?"

"Just to take. Whatever belongs to my wife you can have. She's having an affair. She's cheating on me." The man continued to stand there. He explained to him that there were "her" things and "his" things now, and "their" things, too, and that none of it, nothing in the apartment, was worth keeping. It was just a pile of stuff now, and had to go in one direction or another. A life that had once been, with every added thing, full of hope and purpose, was lost. The man seemed to understand.

He buzzed the man in and heard him on the stairs.

"This place belong to you?"

"It's my apartment," he said. "Go ahead, take what you want. Take whatever you can carry."

The man looked around. "This lamp?" he asked.

The lamp was a "their" thing. What were they going to do, saw it in half? "The lamp's fine," he said. "Take the lamp."

"You sure this stuff is yours?"

"All mine," he said. "Mine and hers."

"This pillow?"

"Take it."

"All these pillows?"

The man headed down the stairs with the lamp and the pillows.

He went back to the window.

An hour later, Katy came down the street.

"You think there's nothing you ain't seen before," one of the men coming toward her said.

"Then you got a guy giving out free luggage," the second man said.

She thought she recognized the polka-dot roller bag that the first man was pulling behind him. When she reached the landing, he was standing in the open doorway, going through the pictures in their wedding album with another woman.

The Stepchild

He circled around again to the bagel place. There was the usual line, but his hope dwindled further with every face that wasn't hers. He went around the block for the dozenth time. After that, he came untethered and wandered south.

Heedless at the corners, he was nearly hit by a cab. He turned right for no reason, and on that block, as he walked, some invisible industrial fan seemed to whir violently, sending up grit and trash. Suddenly, before his eyes, there was an aircraft carrier.

On the outskirts of Times Square he paid the Busking Poetess, dreadlocked and fresh from a stint in Denver, one dollar to peck out a poem on a Smith Corona. He read it for some pressing instruction or sign of relief, but, finding only mock profundity there, he stuck the thing under the windshield of a police cruiser. At the Empire State Building, they tried to get him to take a tour.

There was motion and transition everywhere, the urgent churning city, the cry of a siren fading around the block. Three blue birds suspended before stardust, two astrolabes perched on the gray arms of a wing chair, and a seated shark's jaw all worked together to better display a child's tutu for sale in a shopwindow, before which passersby might have thought him utterly seduced—until he turned and they glimpsed that he was crying. Then they knew they were in one of those city moments, a public audience to a stranger's despair. Long a former smoker, he stopped into the drugstore for cigarettes.

He and Naomi, his wife, had married in Cuba (by way of Nicaragua) four years earlier, long before the embargo was lifted. Nick had thrilled to the risk, the style, of kicking off their days under staid old matrimony in such rebel fashion. There was a priest, and the beach, and the *punto* band, and the northern wind, and everything about that night was emblematic of how they hoped to shape the years. Now they would divorce. Well, of course they would. So what? Sooner or later, everyone got divorced.

Knowing it was useless, she was gone, he threw his cell phone into a mesh bin at the corner. When he came to his senses and returned for it, he searched and searched, but it was no use. He had the wrong corner.

Cyclists yelled at him across the Brooklyn Bridge. He found himself gripping something with fierce resolve. Looking down, he discovered a glossy postcard advertising two-for-one drinks during happy hour at a gentlemen's club. He had no memory of it being handed to him. What did it matter? It was over. Nothing mattered. He walked down Flatbush and into Park Slope.

He had known better than to marry. He'd seen his parents hurt each other, and leave, and hurt and leave others, the casual lovers, the stepparents. But he gave it a shot anyway, and it ended pretty much as he'd imagined, with him wandering the streets in tears.

It was no surprise where he wound up. He hoped to find her there. How he loved her—her face, her smile. He took a deep breath and entered the lobby.

"Who is it?" she asked through an ancient intercom.

"It's Nick," he said, and there followed the longest pause of his life. He had second thoughts. Was he presentable enough? Could he make the right impression? Another minute went by before she buzzed him in.

The elevator, an old cat hibernating on some upper floor, rattled to life when he called it and roared down to him. The doors opened, and he stepped forward with his head down ... and a second later stepped back with his head up, as a family of four charged out—the father first, with the stride of a band leader, then an excitable boy in a Viking hat blasting enemies with a caulk gun, then a German shepherd, then an older brother wearing athletic knee-highs and a soccer jersey as long as a gown, followed at last by Mom, stuck, with her rumpled flannel shirt and sweatpants, in the wrong family in the wrong season, crying out for Bill to be careful with the tomatoes.

"Oh, my God," she said, and stopped and stared. They had switched places: he was inside the elevator, and she was looking at him from the lobby. "I thought that was you." She was gawking. She was tongue tied. "You are just ... awesome."

"Thank you," he said, pressing the button to hurry the door along.

"I mean it—I just love you."

"Thanks."

She finally came to her senses, and a hand shot up to her mouth. "Oh, I'm so embarrassed!" she said. The door began to close. She waved. "Bye!"

On his way up, he put the family out of mind and returned to thinking about her—her face, her smile.

He stepped off the elevator, and there she was, on the phone, propping the apartment door open. One strap of her denim overalls hung off her shoulder, and when she saw him, she smiled happily. Then he neared, and her happiness faded. She palmed the mouthpiece. "Is something wrong?"

"She's gone."

"Who's gone?"

"My wife," he said.

She frowned, waved him in, and hurried to get off the phone.

He moved inside, out of the way of the closing door. He took in the Santa Claus welcome mat many months out of season, the wicker basket against the far wall spilling over with sandals and tennis shoes, the lacquered console table on which the house keys and loose change had been tossed . . . and all the many colors, and vibes, and impressions, and the hundred other ways these perfect strangers chose to live. How many times in the past had he stood like this, on the brink, with the merciless eyes of a child? On, astonishingly, six other occasions, when his parents met other people, and fell in love, and married, and ordered the instant integration of two families' lives, their laundry, and their lore (and, to often disastrous effect, their DNA)—the Morgans, followed by the Dinardos and the Teahans, on his mother's side; the Winklows, the Andersons, and that insufferable Lee clan, on his father's—he had stood like this, appraising and rejecting, and wanting nothing more than to return to the bunk bed in his first room, where all the linens and the wall shadows had been under a single, steady proprietorship. For as soon as his parents were married and moved in, and all the painful adjustments were made, they were divorcing again and moving out.

She apologized for being on the phone. "This will just take another minute," she said.

"Are you alone?" he asked.

She raised a finger and looked away as she wrapped things up with customer service.

A different stranger might have fled, but, as he was easy in unfamiliar surroundings—one of the virtues of his childhood— he made himself at home and continued to take in the state of the apartment. It was a mess. There were toys everywhere, puzzle pieces communing with cereal flakes under the table, and a pink knit blanket on the hardwood floor, which she presently swooped down on with furious efficiency (pocketing the cell phone at last) and folded as they approached the door leading into the next room.

"I can't believe it," she resumed saying. "It's really you!"

"It's really me," he said. "Were you painting?"

"Oh, trying to." She put her finger to her lips. "We have to go through the baby's room to get to the living room," she whispered. "It's the crazy way this apartment was designed. Try not to wake her!"

More clutter awaited them in the living room. The table lamp was on in daylight, and there were cups on top of coasters.

Wheeled toys on leads had been dropped midpull. She hurried to clear a spot for him, heaping stray items on top of a toy bin. He sat down and came up holding a yo-yo.

"So what happened?" she asked.

"She went out this morning for bagels," he said. "We have this routine on Sunday mornings—one of us runs out for bagels and the newspaper, and we spend the morning in bed."

"Oh, my God," she said. "People still do that?"

"But she never came home. I called and I called. She never picked up. She didn't reply to my texts. I waited—I thought maybe she was taking a walk, you know, to clear her head, or whatever. But I don't think so."

"Did you guys have a fight or something?"

"This has been a long time coming," he said.

"I'm sorry to hear that," she said. "Marriage is so hard."

"And, who knows, maybe she is out on a walk."

"How long has it been?"

"Four hours?" he said. "Maybe five?"

"That's kind of a long walk," she said.

He had met her at the arts fund annual gala, in a d.j.'d ballroom in the Paramount Hotel, in Midtown. Two grown women in diapers and pigtails were led around the crowd on a leash before dinner, and men in mascara shook hands with spiky rings on all ten fingers. They were seated next to each other at a table that included Stephanie Savage and Ryan McGinley. She was Calarusso's sometime assistant, there that night to see that the great man ate his soup. During appetizers, Nick learned that she painted in her spare time. By dessert, she was showing him thumbnails of her most recent work and promising to watch his series (if she could find the time to stream it on Netflix). It was not one of the shows that her friends were always telling her she just had to watch.

After the thanks were doled out and the speeches concluded, Calarusso demanded to go home, and she went off to find him a car. The enormous painter, to whom Nick had not been introduced, turned to him and said, with tasteless relish, "The poor girl. She's about to burn her life to the ground and she doesn't even know it."

"What do you mean?"

Calarusso's eyes got wider and gleamed with mischief. "The husband's grown fat."

An hour later, with Calarusso gone, she suddenly confessed that it had been a little more than a million years since she was last out of the house, and she had overdone it. She had had too much to drink and needed to get home.

"Let me drop you off," he said.

"No, it's okay. I can take the subway."

"Don't be silly," he said. "I have a car waiting outside."

He had hoped that they would continue their conversation, but she fell asleep and slept straight through the sudden stops, the thundering starts, the potholes exploding beneath them like mortar bombs. Waiting for her at home, he imagined, was everything anyone could ever want, and she no longer saw much appeal in a stranger. She was above that now. He admired her for it. Her only vice these days? Stolen sleep.

When the car pulled up to her building, he woke her gently, and she opened her eyes and took a deep breath. For a split second, she probably wondered where on earth she was and how she had gotten there.

"I'm sorry," she said. "How long have I been asleep?"

"Since Midtown, more or less."

"Oh, I'm so sorry."

"Don't be," he said.

"Thank you," she said. "You're very sweet."

She said good night and stepped out of the car. That was four days ago.

"I knew it was coming," he said to her now. "I predicted it: eventually, she would leave me. She had to. Day to day, things were just too . . . too . . ."

"What? Awful?"

"Do you know what she does?" he asked incredulously. "First of all, there are flowers. She brings flowers into the house, just to have them around. Then, when they die, instead of just tossing them, she hangs them up to dry and then takes the petals off and puts the petals in these Japanese bowls and then places the bowls here and there around the house."

She waited.

"Who does that?" he asked her.

She laughed in agreement. "I don't know," she said. "I take it you guys don't have kids!"

"No."

"Nobody's drying flowers around here," she said. "Dried flowers wouldn't make it past breakfast."

"And then she makes everything smell nice. There are pleasant little pockets everywhere you go. A little pocket of lemon here in the foyer. A little sachet of lavender near the bathtub. A little candle of verbena in the kitchen. Do you know what that's like?"

"We have pockets like that around here," she said, "but of rotten milk and urine, usually." She laughed.

"I love your apartment," he said.

She looked around, mock startled. "Why?" she asked. She laughed again. "No, it is a nice apartment. It's just too small for us. But rent is so crazy."

"I love how lived in it is."

"Oh, it's lived in, all right. Sometimes it feels like Homer and Langley decided to have children." She picked up a squeeze toy—for a child? a pet?—and made it squeak before tossing it over to a beanbag.

"This is also where you work?"

"Every free minute of every day," she replied.

"You're very driven."

"No," she said. "Just terrified."

"Of?"

"Of never finishing another painting. Of losing myself to motherhood. Of going completely out of my fucking mind."

"I'm so sorry to barge in on you like this," he said. "You're probably trying to get some work done while the baby naps, and here I show up without even calling."

"Please," she said. "I'm happy to see you."

"You have a nice home," he said. "So full of life. Nothing at all like my apartment."

"Where it's clean, you mean? And everything smells nice? And it's quiet? And you can hear yourself think?"

She laughed at herself, or perhaps for his sake, to reassure him, but the mirth drained from her face soon enough, and then she looked around again at the disarray.

"From the outside," she said, "it must look like a pretty good life, like a fulfilled life—which it is. But when you're plunked down in the middle of it, sometimes it just feels like time fleeing."

"I love you," he said.

She pulled back. "Pardon?"

"No, just this life, I mean. Your apartment. The mess, even. I love the...I really love rooms like this one, where you can practically hear the children playing, and the washing machine going, and you can smell the banana bread baking in the oven. You really feel the love in this room, that's all I meant. You and your husband have three kids, is that right?"

She nodded.

"Where is he now?"

But she had gone silent.

She was the real thing. He could not simply say "I love you" and look at her until she melted. Calarusso was wrong. She had resolve, and self-respect. She would not just run off with the latest man who flattered her, as his mother had done, taping the children up for transport in a used box, to test the advantages of a different address.

"Listen, I'm sorry," he said. "I didn't mean to give you the wrong impression. Naomi—that's my wife—she's not some insane person who needs to have everything perfectly in place all the time. Our apartment gets plenty messy. But let me tell you something she does do without fail every day. She makes the bed. Now, I wasn't taught to make the bed every day. Some of my stepparents hated that about me, and I didn't make the bed on purpose half the time just to get back at them. But then I got married, and for some reason, I'd look at the bed Naomi had made and I'd see, you know, not kindness, not...whatever. I'd see spite! I'd think she'd made the bed deliberately to criticize me, or to prove how much more considerate she was than me, or some other stupid thing, and I resented her for it. For making the bed! We'd get into these fights, I'd bring up the bed, she'd look at me like, 'What are you talking about? What does making the bed have to do with anything?' And then, one day, it just dawned on me. She's not making the bed to get back at me. She's making the bed because she likes a made bed. She wants our lives, our shared life together, to be pleasant. I had never thought about that before, the fact that I had a shared life."

"You should have kids," she said. "Then you know it's shared."

"I was telling you about how my apartment smells good," he said. "Well, when I was a kid, right, and into my teens, and into my twenties, even, I was surrounded—this will sound weird, now that I'm about to say it out loud—by all of these strange people's smells, the different odors of different families. I mean the soaps they had in their bathrooms. Their coat closets, their family recipes. The breath their sofas let out when you sat down on them. And then the grosser things—how they left the bathroom, what they gave off when you got too close. It wasn't always repugnant, just foreign, and I didn't want the foreign. I wanted the familiar. That's what family is: what's familiar. And every new house I went to, every new family I joined, they had all these scents that weren't familiar. I could no longer say what would have been familiar. I just knew that it was nowhere present in those houses. So when Naomi and I got married, and I had to adjust to a whole new set of scents—and, you know, things, possessions, wall hangings, whatever—I was just like, no. What was the point of being married if I just had to keep adjusting? I wouldn't do it, I refused. In my head, I mean. Those were Naomi's things, not mine. What was mine? I had no idea, really. I just knew, in my head, I would not give in. So we fought. We fought like cats and dogs. Until one day I realized that her scents had become my scents. They were my scents. This was my life. Why was I sabotaging it? I finally knew what was mine."

He stopped talking. She narrowed her eyes and looked at him intently. "Huh," she said. Something in his monologue had provoked her. She looked away. She even stood up, crossed her arms, and started to pace back and forth. She seemed to have forgotten entirely about his blurting out that he loved her. She came to a stop and said, "It's the exact opposite with me."

"How so?"

"Well, I used to have my own odors—that's a funny way of putting it. You know what I mean. My own life. But it's the kids' life now, it's the kids' odors. They've blotted everything else out. God only knows what I smell like now." He expected her to laugh, but she didn't. It wasn't meant to be a joke. "Do you know how hard it is some days just to find time to take a shower and put on lotion? Will I ever take a bath again? I don't know. Will I ever smell of perfume again? Will I ever paint something that's worth a damn?"

"What does your husband say?" he asked.

"About what?"

He wasn't sure, and shrugged. "Your painting. Your desire to take a bath."

"He and I have our ups and downs," she said. "Like any couple."

Returning to the sofa, she folded the white onesie that had suddenly appeared in her hands, setting it down absentmindedly on a pile of children's books. "Anyway," she said.

"It's worse now," he said. "I might have been better off never figuring it out."

"Figuring what out?"

"What's mine."

"That's worse than not knowing?"

"Perfect terror," he said.

"Why?"

"Because now I know what I have to lose."

He had returned to the fact of Naomi's abandonment and all the loss he had suffered when she hadn't come back to the apartment that morning.

"It's more than just a made bed," he said. "We talked, the two of us. We shared things. No one in my family ever talked. They shouted, they slammed doors, and then they filed for divorce. My mother had one of her wedding receptions in a McDonald's. That's how casual these things were. But Naomi and me, we made dinner together every night I wasn't on set. We planned things. We did things."

"And now that's over?"

"Over completely."

"But you loved her."

"I did, yes, very much. I never used to live for my life. I lived to prove something, and to get revenge. But my life was a small, mean thing. Then, somewhere along the way, it became everything. That was terrifying."

"But beautiful, too," she said, fingering her wedding ring. "Not sure I do that."

"You don't live for your life?"

"I don't know what I live for," she said. "I live to neglect the other half of things."

"What's the other half of things?"

"Well, for instance. When I'm painting, I'm not taking care of my kids. And when I'm taking care of my kids, I'm not painting. That pretty much guarantees that I don't do either very well, and every night I sort of hate myself for it."

"And your husband?" he said. "What do you neglect when you're with him?"

"Calarusso, for one," she said. "And other things. Friends. Museums. Life." She laughed.

"He doesn't like museums?"

"It isn't that he doesn't like them," she said. "It's that we never go to them. If we do anything together, it's watch TV. You probably don't watch TV, do you? Oh, that's a stupid question—you're on TV. But you know what I mean. With your wife. When you're both tired. As the thing two people do. To be together."

"I know what you mean," he said. "But, no, Naomi preferred to do other things. Dinners, plays. She was with me on Corsica last year when I was filming this absolutely terrible independent movie, and I remember we got out of the car and walked down these ancient crumbling stairs to the beach, and we had this long swim, but when we came back, the car was surrounded by all of these wild boars. Rutting like crazy—it was really funny. But scary, too, you know? This man from Marseille began honking his horn and somehow led them away. We'd still be there to this day if it weren't for him."

She didn't seem to know how to respond to this story. "Sounds romantic," she said.

"Romantic?"

"I just mean Corsica."

"Oh, I guess it was," he said. "But, you know, looking back, it wasn't the travel we did. It was the fact that we were polite to each other. Where I come from, no one was ever polite. If I'm being honest, she taught me how to live."

"This is a mortal woman we're talking about, right?"

He laughed. "Oh, look," he said. "She had her flaws, trust me."

"Like?"

He gave the question some thought. "She doesn't have nearly the sense of humor you do," he said. "Or the richness."

"Richness?"

He didn't know how to answer, and the question hung in the air. She got to her feet again, walked to the middle of the room, and with her back to him stood thinking.

"She sounds amazing," she said at last, "and you should fight for her. Wherever she is, find her and fight for her. For your sake."

"But it's too late," he said. "We exhausted something, working through it. You try to make it work, but something gets ruined along the way. I tried her patience too many times. There's nothing I could say now, and nothing I could do."

"You have to beg her. You have to vow to change, and then change."

"I have changed. Completely. She just doesn't see it. To her, I'll always be that bratty kid who couldn't bring himself to make the necessary adjustments. Do you know how easy it is to get pigeonholed by the person you're married to, and then you just can't get out of it?"

"Oh, God, yes," she said.

"That doomed us. We were always going to be the same

people to each other, no matter how much we changed." He gestured around the apartment. "I never considered her capable of any of this, for instance."

"Any of what?" she asked. "The mess? The madness?"

"No, no," he said. "The...the nurture. The wholeness of your lives. How there's goodness behind every little thing in sight. Your husband must feel the same way."

"Oh, sure," she said. "He can't shut up about all the goodness. He's always romancing me for everything he finds on the living room floor. Are you kidding me?"

"The minute I walked in," he said, "I thought, Here is how life is best lived. Everywhere you look, there's a sign of life. And you created it. It's amazing. It's like...like a garden in here. No, hear me out," he said when she had raised her eyebrows skeptically. "And what you are growing here, and there, and over there, are little moments, and the little moments make your memories, and the memories make a life that can't be taken away from you by anyone or anything, not other people's fickleness, not even death. In the long run, you know, that's better than bowls of dried flowers, or whatever."

"I don't know," she said. "I'm pretty intrigued by those bowls."

When he had finished, she came back to the sofa, curled one leg under her and sat down, looking at him with (he thought) a sexy pucker to her mouth, eyes narrowed, and held his gaze a beat longer than was strictly necessary.

"And what about love?" she asked.

"Love is everywhere in this house," he said. "Everywhere."

"I don't mean that kind of love," she said. "Don't be seduced by the children's toys."

"What do you mean?"

"What do you mean, what do I mean? I mean love. I mean . . . what *do* I mean? Okay, it's like this," she said. "Do you see that toy over there? It's some kind of caped lion. But also a digital clock. I'm not really sure what the hell it is, to be honest. But when Micah—that's my oldest—when Micah first got that caped lion–clock thing, it was everything to him. I mean, it was the most precious jewel on earth. He went around all day hugging it to his chest. But now he never plays with it. Ever. You know what he plays with?"

She plucked off the floor a spent roll of toilet paper with a twisted rubber band taped to it. "This."

He laughed.

"I'm not joking."

She waggled the toilet roll, and the strap of her overalls fell off her shoulder again.

"And that's what my husband has become to me, and what I have become to my husband. He and I both remember, sort of, way back before kids, that we had something, but in all honesty now, after the kids go to bed, we go right back to playing with our toilet rolls. Oh, my God," she said. "I can't believe that just came out of my mouth."

"And what is your husband's toilet roll?"

"His iPhone," she said without hesitation.

"And yours?"

"Whatever I'm painting at the moment," she said. "You worry about losing everything. I worry about wanting to hold on to it. Some days, I don't know if I have the strength to hold on to it."

"You're unhappy," he said.

She was forced to look away but turned back quickly and looked at him as if she were seeing him there for the first time. "How did you get in here?" she asked him, smiling. "Did I let you in?" He remained still, staring at her with his chin lowered, a faint smile curling the ends of his mouth. "It must be those eyes," she said, more quietly than before. "Those eyes are hard to say no to."

So she was susceptible, after all. She was not what the state of her apartment had suggested: a mother through and through, and had not fallen asleep on their ride into Brooklyn because she was above it all. Calarusso had not been wrong.

His disappointment in her was sharp but brief, and bound up with excitement. He reached across the sofa and slowly lifted the denim strap to her shoulder. "Maybe I should be going," he whispered.

She nodded. "Maybe you should."

Neither of them moved.

"I can't seem to bring myself to."

"Seems you can't."

"The truth is, I want to stay."

"Why?" she whispered. "Is it all the sippy cups?"

He smiled. "No."

"The wide selection of Little Golden Books?"

"It's you," he said. "It's this. It's all of this."

"I'm flattered."

"I'm serious."

"But you're still in love with your wife," she said. "Aren't you?"

He would always love her, he admitted. But it had been so much worse in days past, when he drifted, crying, down dead industrial blocks, and strangers removed their earbuds to ask him if he was all right. Oh, yes, it had been much worse in times past. This morning was an afterthought, a fainthearted performance, the death rattle, and when he came to his senses, what had he done? Walked straight over the bridge to her.

"This is the life I want!" he said. "I want you!"

"Are you sure it's me," she asked, "and not some fantasy you've constructed around my life?"

Then he told her that there was a woman who kept recurring in his dreams. "She shows up every few months, always while I'm in transit. I'm on a boat, or an airplane, and she just happens to be seated next to me. We talk, and then she looks at me, and I wake up. I'm always sad to wake up. I've had this dream for twenty-five years, ever since I was a kid, and I've always just believed that she was a figment of my imagination. Until I sat down next to you at dinner four nights ago."

"We weren't in transit."

"I drove you home."

"Does that count?"

"I'm counting it. And do you remember the name of the painting Calarusso auctioned that night?"

"Across the Waters to Saint-Tropez."

"While we were on the bridge, a favorite song of mine came on the radio. An old song called 'San Tropez.' "

"Hey, I know that song," she said. She sang the first two lines. "That one?"

" 'And you're leading me down to the place by the sea,' " he sang. "That's the one."

They shared another look, and then she kissed him. After the first few tentative kisses, she crossed a leg over his lap and straddled him.

When they broke off, she looked at him from only a few inches away.

"Oh, my God," she said. And she suddenly threw her head back and laughed. "This isn't happening."

"Yes," he said. "It is."

They kissed again and afterward began a series of goodbyes, for her husband would be home from the park soon with the boys and the dog in tow, and everyone would be hot and cranky and in need of a snack, and it would be better, she said to him, thinking vaguely of the future, that he not be seen, not known, yet. They had every intention of getting up from the sofa but remained there, kissing more freely now, and between kisses he shared with her more of his childhood and recommended that no one act too rashly, for the sake of the children.

"No, yeah, of course. No one's going to...no one's doing anything stupid," she said. "But, listen..."

"What?"

"Well, I don't know," she said. "I just...I just know that I have to paint, that's all."

"Of course you do," he said. "Always. We'll make sure of it."

Was that what she meant? Or did she mean right now, she needed to paint right now? Had he overplayed his hand? No— she was smiling, nodding. They were on the same wavelength, thank God.

Another ten minutes passed, and now it was imperative that she send him on his way. But they stole another minute, and when they left off kissing again, she backtracked, saying it could never work out between them, because he was used to an apartment that smelled nice, where you could read the paper over bagels on a Sunday morning, and not a pigsty where toys were scattered everywhere.

"But I can't live like that anymore," he said. "It's too precious. I need a good mess."

"That's too bad," she said, "because I wouldn't mind a little verbena in my life."

"Oh, well, that I can do," he said.

Then it was time, they had to get up, and four daring and exquisite minutes later they did. Holding hands this time, they returned through the baby's room to the front door. The baby stirred, then let out a cry—and then it didn't matter how carefully she shut the door behind her. Nap time was over. "Shit," she said.

"Go," he said. "Take care of him. I'll see myself out."

"It's a her," she said, and they kissed a final time. He was halfway out the door when she called him back and hurried across the room.

"Maybe I should just tell him," she said.

"Tell who?"

"My husband," she said. "Doesn't he deserve to know?"

"What would you tell him?"

She thought about it. "I don't know," she said, and caught herself. "What's even happening?"

"Nothing," he said. "And everything. Maybe you should. I don't know—whatever you think is best."

She leaned in to him to steal one final kiss. Then he left the apartment and walked toward the elevator, which disgorged an unhappy man, two hot and sullen boys, and a Jack Russell terrier panting from the heat.

He had arrived there in the depths of despair but was leaving now wordless with joy. At the station, he realized again that he didn't have his wallet and had to jump the turnstile. He wanted to text her, or call her, for some reassurance—and to recapitulate every sentiment of the past hour and then, as the conversation meandered, to exchange the bolder impressions that each must have of the other, which could come spilling out now that they had broken through to a level of intimacy. Ah, what happiness! To have found her at last, someone who would never leave! But he couldn't text or call, because he had thrown away his phone.

The doorman loaned him a spare key, but it must not have been the right one or something, because, though it slid inside the lock just fine, it wouldn't turn. He was about to give up when he heard footsteps, and a few seconds later the door opened from the inside. Surprised, he stood upright.

"Oh," he said. "You're home."

His wife turned on high-arched feet and padded away soundlessly, disappearing into the bedroom. He stood there a minute with the door open, feeling the cool, settled calm of the rooms filling up with dusk. After turning and shutting the door, he remained standing there a minute longer. Finally, he shuffled across the apartment and stood on the brink of the bedroom, looking in. She was packing an overnight bag that lay open on the bed.

"You thought I had left," she said.

He nodded, looking sheepish.

"But you see now I didn't." She dropped a camisole on the bed and held up her arms. "How many times, Nick?"

"I really did think you were gone this time," he said.

"I don't doubt that," she said. She turned to the dresser, but only to stand there at an open drawer, stirring things around uncertainly.

"You're not leaving now, are you?"

"What choice do I have? We've talked about this and talked about it," she said, sounding tired. "I thought we were making progress."

"We were," he said. "We are."

"And your cell phone?"

He shook his head.

"You call that progress?" She shook her head, so full of disappointment in him. "I ran into Trish at the bagel place," she explained. "Charles is going back to Texas. No one will say a word to Marie about the baby. And then she tells me that she and Teddy are getting married and she wants me to be her maid of honor. Before I know it, we're in that little bridal shop around the corner. I just lost track of time. That's it, Nick. That's all."

"I tried to call you."

"My phone was here!"

"I kept texting you."

"I was just running out for bagels!"

Exasperated, she sat down on the bed. Feeling stupid, he drifted away.

Not long after, from the guest bedroom, he saw the light go on in the kitchen. He heard her taking things down from the shelves. The refrigerator door opened and closed. A minute later, she began to chop. When something hit the pan and sizzled—he pictured her running her finger down the length of the blade, sliding the garlic into the hot oil—he was reminded of what, in fact, was best in life. It was Naomi's garlic crackling, the smell filling the apartment, and the bottle of wine she would open. That beat all else, the garlic and the wine, hands down. Could she blame him for going out of his mind at the thought of it ending?

He walked to the kitchen and stood in the doorway gloomily and waited for her to speak.

"Who was it this time?" she asked finally, without looking up.

He shrugged. "Someone I met at the gala."

She lifted her head. To look at him, she had to move the hair out of her eyes, which she did awkwardly, with the wrist of the hand holding the knife. "You just abandon me, Nick," she said. "I never know where you've gone."

"I never really go anywhere," he said.

"You drive me so crazy," she said.

But then she sighed, and the fight left her body. Still shaking her head in dismay, she allowed a little smile. Without another word, he stepped into the kitchen and pulled down his own knife, and took up an onion and began to chop. He chopped for his life, hoping to be forgiven by the time dinner was served.

Life in the Heart of the Dead

Gray skies. A silver tray of individually wrapped cheeses. Bad coffee in boardrooms. That was Prague to me, that "city of a hundred spires." And I might have boarded the plane knowing nothing more had Antonin not turned to me during that final dinner and said, "If you are free tomorrow, perhaps we go on walking tour?"

Mop-brush mustache, bald head brown as a liver. Was he with the embassy? He was with us for at least two of those endless meals. The tourism bureau?

I did not want to go on a walking tour. But I was boozy and delirious from lack of sleep and didn't know how to decline with any grace. "Great idea. But let's not do anything before ten o'clock."

Jet lag. It is never the hours you don't sleep, but all the years that seem to have passed since you last felt awake, that make it so unbearable. I woke like a lightbulb at three in the morning, ready to shower and get on the highway. But I wasn't in Cleveland. I was in Prague, and the only one alive. I lay there feeling sorry for myself, and a little frightened, until a glow appeared at the edges of the curtains.

I didn't know a thing about Prague when I arrived at Václav Havel Airport. I don't know anything about it now. We lost our pitch to the Dutch and moved on to Montreal, where we did better than expected until the most recent downturn. If you asked me what Prague was like, I'd tell you about the Costa Coffee down the street from my hotel, where the coffee was hot and the Wi-Fi decent.

One night, hoping to restore my sleep, I tried jogging. I ran down Ostrovní Street in the dark and crossed over to the river-bank. For half a mile I saw one car only, a lonely taxicab. Was it four in the morning? Or two, or three? The road forked, and I went down a service drive to the water. I was told the market there on Sunday mornings was lively, but I didn't see a soul. I passed empty riverboats and rusted barges. The lights along the cobblestone path strained against the darkness. I was short of breath. I felt old and fat. I took a seat on a rain-logged bench. Dark waters. Still boats. The suggestion of beauty, if only I could see past the terror. Would anyone notice if I just keeled over?

So that was a bust. Still, I took my time getting back to the hotel. There was a man there who made me uneasy. An employee of the place, frighteningly tall. A giant, in fact.

I have a shallow understanding. I don't like to admit it, but there you go.

At dinner one night, I was seated next to a woman from the embassy. She was a Czech native, fluent in about a hundred languages. A stalwart blond, of middle age or more, with fat fingers and a sallow complexion. I could just picture her during Communism, in gray coveralls, singing the workers' chorus and hating the West. But in fact she'd been a resistance fighter and a signatory and a whatever else.

What I remember best about this woman, whose name is long gone, had to do with a flower. She had been the one to greet us at the embassy when we arrived for a tour. We went through a courtyard and up the steps to the first of three terraced gardens. Two groundsmen in matching jumpsuits were out on the lawn, one peering into the tank of his lawn mower. I was sleep deprived, already winded and ready to move on (but to what?). I thought going up that hill just to come back down again was a total waste of time (better served how?).

At the top, we stood on a pavilion taking in a panoramic view. Everyone *ooh*ed and *aah*ed. Directly before me, red gabled rooftops were huddled together like knockabout boats in a crowded harbor. Eventually we started down again. The woman from the embassy—I was now behind her in line—was naming the flowers as we went, complimenting the groundsmen for keeping the gardens beautiful, when suddenly she swooped down on a tulip or whatever and plucked it. I was shocked. Wasn't that breaking the rule—if not a formal one of the embassy's, then one shared by us all—about leaving helpless little flowers in the fucking ground? I wondered what she'd do with it now that it was hers. Would she take it inside, put it in some water?

She gave it a whiff and tossed it aside. It landed on the lawn and began to die. Life was cheap. It scared the shit out of me.

Anyway, we were eight (ten? twelve?) at dinner a few nights

later, when I found myself seated next to her. There was a castle outside the window, a really big one. Black as a void, terrible looking. First time I'd noticed it. Was that *the* castle? And what did I mean by that, *the* castle? Was there a moat? Were there dungeons where the worst of the medieval tortures took place? Were they taking place still? Did people live there, work there? What had the Communists done with the castle when they were in power? All week I'd gone around asking what the Communists had done with this and what the Communists had done with that. Where had the Communists bought their hand luggage, how had the Communists opened their wine?

"Hey, tell me something," I said to the woman from the embassy. "What is that?"

She stared at the castle through the window as if noticing it for the first time, too. When she turned back, she cocked her head at me and said, "You've been here for three days now, and you still don't know what that is?"

"Looks like a castle," I said.

"It's *Prague* Castle," she said. "And by the way," she added, just when the whole table, and really the whole restaurant, seemed to go completely silent. "For some reason, you keep calling it Czechoslovakia. You understand, I hope, that it isn't Czechoslovakia anymore. It hasn't been Czechoslovakia for twenty years. It's the Czech Republic now. If you really hope to"—she searched for the right phrase—"blanket the city with billboards, you might want to keep that in mind."

Someone dropped a fork on a plate. Then Baxter, my second-in-command, said in a loud voice, "Anyone for dessert?"

An hour later, our little group parted out on the street. "Try to take an interest in things," she advised me.

Jesus Christ—what the hell sort of thing was that to say to a person? She really hated me, I think.

I don't know where I got the idea—Ohio, probably—that I had nothing to fear in Prague. But after parting from my colleagues and returning to the hotel alone, I got lost inside a maze of foreign streets, all dimly lit and scarred with tram tracks, from which I could have easily disappeared without a trace. As I tried to find my way out again, it struck me that my safety was simply a matter of luck—the luck of the times. An official representative of the state had found me offensive. From as little as that there might have followed, in a different era, surveillance, menace, and death.

But back to Antonin.

I woke up the morning of our tour feeling terrible. Did I need to vomit, or was I just hungry? What I really needed was a dozen strong cups of hot coffee. Then I remembered what I had agreed to. I groaned and fell back in bed. See, I'm not just shallow. I'm lazy, too. I didn't give a damn about Prague. I'd see it next time. And if there was no next time? Even better.

But I was too lazy to cancel, and an hour later, when Antonin called up to my room, I had no choice but to drag-ass it down to the lobby.

"How did you sleep?" he asked, rising from a drab wing chair. Tweed suit coat, no tie, taller than I remembered. No longer young, but trim and handsome.

Who *was* he? He might have known how I fit in, but I had no clue who he was or why he was sacrificing a Saturday morning to parade me around the city.

"Like the damned," I replied.

He smiled. Then his amusement faded and he furrowed his brow. "Do you mean . . . like the dead?"

Yes! That was it—the dead. But I liked my version better. I had slept like the damned, the *soon-to-be* dead, and told him that was what I meant.

"Doesn't sound good," he said.

"No," I agreed, "but if I get some coffee in me, who knows, I might just live."

The desk clerk had stepped away. There was no one to take my room key except the giant. He was seven and a half feet tall if he was an inch, the sort of man you turn to have a second look at when he walks by you in the street. The sort of man who plays freaks and henchmen in the movies, who in real life becomes a porter in a hotel.

"Can I leave this with you?" I asked him.

He came around the counter with great reluctance, ducking his head as a matter of course, as other men do only inside airplanes. He had the floppy blond hair of a skateboarder and a mousy little mustache. He took the golden key from my hand and hung it up, then turned back to stare cadaverously at me across the counter. I had the urge to request he give the key back just to make him do it, but there was a little voice: "Don't provoke a man of that size!"

Out on the street, I said to Antonin, "I don't think he likes me."

"Who—the golem?"

I laughed. "Yes—whatever that is. He thinks I take advantage of your women."

"Oh?"

I gave Antonin an abbreviated version of the incident I had

in mind. Two nights earlier, awake and restless, I'd left my room for a smoky pub just down Ostrovní, where I made conversation with a woman at the bar. I returned to the hotel a few hours later with my new friend. When we entered, I detected a look from the giant: "Ah, here we go, another asshole adulterer." (With Antonin, I kept that fact to myself.) But how could the giant know I was married? No, it was just a look of old-fashioned jealousy. The giant was duty bound and bored at his lonely post, while the American was heading upstairs with a woman.

I did tell Antonin the worst part—for the giant, that is. He made the night possible, as she put her fingertips on the small of my back, when he was forced to hand over my room key.

We took a left, then a right, then another left...or maybe a right and then a left. Either way, I was lost in no time and at Antonin's complete mercy.

"We don't do a lot of walking in Cleveland," I told him. "Easier just to drive everywhere."

"Hmm," he said. "Yes. Gas guzzlers."

"I don't suppose there are any sights you'd like to see by car, are there?"

"Better to go on foot, I think. Is it okay?"

"Sure," I said. "It is a walking tour, after all. But should we stop for coffee first?"

"Best coffee in Prague is on same route I take us," he said. "Trust me, you don't want this Starbucks."

He made a sour face and pointed.

Because there it was, in among the stalls and chintz shops on that cobblestone street: a spanking-new Starbucks! And yet we made no move to stop, to enter, to order! It was getting away! Were we out of our minds?

Well, when in Rome. Here we come, best cup in Prague. Though just then I would have happily chugged cold Folgers from a gas can.

One thing became clear. Antonin didn't take his guiding duties lightly. We started in the town square, and within two minutes he was gushing facts: dates, names, conflicts, invasions, cruel deaths. I stood there feeling self-conscious. When he didn't stop, it dawned on me. This wasn't just some casual stroll through Prague. It was a damned history lesson! Antonin and I were going to go deep while standing upright! My heart sank. I wasn't in the mood. The guidebooks tell you to soak up the history, but that stuff just beads on the surface and runs right off me. Here's all I knew about history. Year after year in Cleveland public school, the teachers trotted out the same two events—the Boston Tea Party followed by the Gettysburg Address—and there did dull dead history start and stop.

Antonin turned and began to walk backward over the cobblestones, beckoning for me to follow as if I were a group of Japanese tourists.

"And here we have very famous statue of Jan Hus," he said, "reformist cleric from fifteenth century who, as you may know, was first to—"

But I knew nothing and let my mind wander until he said something that caught my attention.

"Wait a minute—isn't that just a figure of speech?"

"No."

"He was literally burned at the stake?"

"Yes."

"This guy here?"

I pointed, and Antonin nodded. Tall and thin as a Czech Abraham Lincoln, the martyr before us made an ugly statue. I studied his face. With the exception of the moral courage etched there, and the divine purpose in his bearing, he was a man no different from me. Happy to be home, he takes off his shoes and wiggles his toes in front of the fire, when suddenly there's a knock at the door. Next thing he knows, he's tied to a stake and his toes are smoking, fucking *smoking*.

"His poor toes," I said.

Antonin looked at me uncertainly and smiled. "Shall we go to cathedral now?"

"What cathedral?"

He pointed to a dome in the distance. It seemed a long way to walk just for a church.

"Do we have to walk?"

"Pardon?"

"Seems far to me. What do you think? I guess we could walk it."

We walked it. A half hour later, I was running for the exit.

"What the fuck is a human bone doing nailed to the inside of that church?"

"Forearm of thief," he explained. "A man who is stealing all the golds of the Madonna, so—" He made a terrible noise—it was half–table saw, half–wrung neck—as he ripped an imaginary forearm from an imaginary thief.

"Was this recent?"

"No, long time ago in history."

"This is why I don't have anything to do with history," I

said. "People fall into the wrong hands and just get eaten alive. Martyr, thief, it makes no difference. It could happen to anybody, even a nobody like me. No, thanks. Better to stay locked inside the hotel."

He laughed. "But what is happening then to participation?"

"Participation in what?"

He gestured. "The world."

He hauled me under the shadow of the astronomical clock—not a real shadow but a palpable gloom. Drab pigeons flew across the clock face, which was fastidiously hampered with fancy orbs and dials. He launched into another spiel. I fell asleep a tiny bit standing up, like some kind of horse.

"Wait," I said, jerking awake. "The clock maker was blind?"

"No, was blinded," he said, "by very jealous city elders of Prague, who are wanting him never to build another clock like this one anywhere else."

"What do you mean, blinded?"

He told me what he meant.

"Fuck me!" I cried. "That happens?"

"Excuse me," a woman's voice said in just about the most perfect English imaginable. "Do you mind keeping your voice down? There are children."

She wasn't kidding. She had about ten of them all around her.

"Oh, sorry," I said. "Jeez, you don't expect that to happen to you in Prague."

"Shall we stay for show?" he asked, explaining that some grand performance took place at the top of every hour.

"That depends," I said. "Do they come around with coffee?"

A minute later, saints of some kind began to rotate in an

upper window while figures of vice, like Death and the money-lender, leered at us from a lintel. It was a cautionary tale and primitive animatronics show. The crowd cheered. They raised their iPhones and digital cameras, a hideous beast of a hundred limbs, to record it all and prove they'd been to Prague. If I had been Death looking down on us, I would have been frightened out of my mind.

A few minutes later my attention was captured by the many young men on Segways in that square soliciting tourists to go for a spin. Remember those early boasts about the Segway, how it was supposed to forever alter the history of human transportation? Well, now it's just another thing blighting the tourist traps of the earth, alongside the pigeons and fanny packs.

"I bet the Communists wouldn't have allowed Segways in this town square," I said. "Bet they had more self-respect than that."

"Yes, they would have forbidden it as capitalist tool."

"That would suggest that it's somehow useful."

A dark-skinned young man in a blue tuxedo had a pair of old ladies on the hook. Too old, I thought, to be doing anything on a Segway. Nevertheless, a minute later, the stouter of the two was handing off her purse to the taller one and climbing aboard. She'd clearly lost her mind. Looking down at her feet, groping blindly for the control bar, she just barely managed to get on. I thought for sure the man would come to his senses and call it off, but he only seemed to be encouraging her.

"You've got to be kidding me," I said.

Both Antonin and I were watching when the man finally let go. That old lady glided forward easy-peasy for about five feet, then veered violently to the left and headed straight for a couple licking ice cream cones while looking down at a map. They barely managed to glance up just before she walloped them, and I mean *walloped* them. They tumbled, and the old lady just went flying. They climbed to their feet and dusted themselves off. Not so the old lady. She was still lying on the pavement when Antonin and I descended into the dungeon.

"Know what that was?" I asked him.

He didn't, and looked at me inquiringly.

"Participation in the world," I said.

Upon our return, the old lady was laid out on a gurney and being loaded up into the back of an ambulance. A peal of siren replaced the general pall, and slowly the ambulance coasted out of sight. The crowd dispersed, and the day resumed.

"You know a lot about Prague," I said on our way out of that square at last.

"Well, I hope so," he said.

"I was just wondering what I could tell you about Cleveland. There isn't much. How to avoid the toll roads, and where to get your shirts cleaned."

He smiled. "That can be important."

"You know a lot about history, too. What do you do for a living, Antonin? I must have known at one point, but it's slipped my mind."

"Call me Tony," he said. "I am tour guide."

"You're what? A tour guide?"

"Well," he said. "We are on tour, yes?"

I laughed. "You're a tour guide?"

"Yes."

"An actual guide!"

"Yes!"

"How did you...?"

"Get involved with your group? The embassy is arranging it," he said. "But I don't work for embassy. Here." He removed a business card from the inside pocket of his suit coat. It read: ANTONIN MALIC, PRAGUE WALKING TOURS.

A tour guide! With part delirium, part delight, I began to laugh. Tears came to my eyes. I had to stop walking so I could double over and howl until I went mute. Was it really all that funny? Maybe only I thought so. But how good it was to laugh like that. Ruin was over. Insomnia was past. And when I looked up again, I saw Antonin, I mean really saw him, for the first time. He was smiling helplessly along with me. An honest-to-God guide!

In the Old Town, where the medieval streets were tall and twisting, Death continued to be the star attraction. But the crowd quickly got to me, my laughing jag was a thing of the past, and I was eager to get a move on. Where to, exactly? No idea. This was Tony the Tour Guide's show. But I was determined to get there first.

What was wrong with me? Here's what I feared would happen one day. After a lifetime spent in a hurry, I'd wake up and realize that there was never any destination, life was all tour, and in a paradox beyond comprehension, some more real destination would be revealed, one I could never have dreamed of, and at last I'd see that I had come in dead last.

On Karlova Street, down which a cab had ventured for a fare, the crowd was so thick that the poor driver was at a standstill. I was behind Tony when I saw my chance. I halted, then swung around the rear of the car while he continued ahead of me, oblivious. One last look and I ducked into a café.

The steely stormtrooper behind the counter lined up four espressos on the worm-eaten bar, and I downed them one after another.

It was an awful thing to do. As the coffee was being prepared, Antonin was negotiating his way through a thick crowd, only to look back and find me gone. No doubt he stopped and scanned the crowd in a growing panic. All so that I could indulge myself. If his tour so far had taught me anything at all, it was that throughout history, some people acted nobly. Me, I had never loved anyone but myself.

I didn't mind once the espressos took effect. I left a fat American tip and skipped out of there.

"Tony!" I cried.

He was standing in the street with his back against the brick wall, doing his best to pick me out of the crowd. "I don't know what happened," he said.

"Well, we're together now." In my euphoria, I briefly took his arm. "Let's go see all the rest of the immortal things, Tony, what do you say? Take me to all the very best spots!"

Let history unfurl. Let the savages kill. For the rest of us, there is the art of living well in a dangerous world.

We pulled up before an open-air market. Still high as a kite on my four espressos, I found my will to live again and peppered him with questions.

"Were these stalls we see here today around during the Communist era?"

"Yes, as matter of fact."

"And were they selling the same things?"

"Of course, not everything," he said. "Today this market is very touristical."

"And were you giving tours back then?"

He had been leading tours through Prague, he told me, for thirty years, since the late eighties, when his audience consisted of Soviet architects, party apparatchiks, contingents of vacationing East Germans.

"Was your tour a lot different for those folks?"

"How meaning different?"

"Did you tailor it to a Communist audience? Were there, I don't know, fewer churches and more...steelworks, or whatever?"

"Still people are wanting to see churches," he said. "No, I must say, it was same tour."

"Was there anything under Communism that was better than it is today?"

"Better?" he said. "Under Communism?" He gave me an emphatic frown as he shook his head. "Absolutely nothing."

Then I wanted it to be over. The caffeine wore off, and I wanted to go home. I was on some bridge—the greatest bridge in the world, according to Antonin. What was so great about it, other than providing an opportunity to jump?

Everywhere we'd gone that day, bronze plaques kept popping up to mark some historic occasion. Here resistance fighters had dug a tunnel, here the dissidents had withstood the tanks. The whole city was like that: one giant monument to the heroes and martyrs. But what about those of us just trying to get by? I put on my sunglasses and stared out at the water.

In the distance was the riverbank I had run down a few nights earlier. There was the bench where I'd sat at three in the morning, trying to catch my breath. If I had keeled over that night, as I'd feared, what would I have left behind? It was plain as day: nothing. No flowery memorial would have marked the spot, certainly no bronze plaque. I might as well kill myself, I thought. Why not? What did my life amount to? What had I done to make a difference? Ah, but I was forgetting. Thanks to me, there were billboards, hundreds of them, in fact, some promoting nothing more than their own availability. I liked to tell myself that the terror that stalked me in Prague was the terror of being sent for, hunted down, caught in the crosshairs of history. But my terror in the light of day wasn't of that sort at all. It was the terror of failing to even merit the attention. I was a speck of dust.

Everyone knows it's important to be on the right side of history. But I had the sudden sense, vertiginous, awful: *it didn't matter*. Tell me the difference between the heroism of the martyrs and the perfidy of the traitors once death has leveled them both at last? Perhaps if evil were vanquished, if the virtuous took evil down with them—if, somewhere in Prague, there stood plaques that said "Here lies murder," "Here lies war," "Here lies brute force"...but there were no such plaques and never would be. The world was a continuing shit show despite the innumerable heroes and martyrs. Why had I even gotten out of bed?

Here I should introduce the good Dr. Haymark and convey

his opinion that it was time to give the antidepressants a try. But I didn't need drugs. I needed to get the fuck out of Prague. This kind of provocation was entirely missing in Cleveland, where there were Dunkin' Donuts, outdoor malls, and a sports arena with an enormous parking lot. You never had to think about shit like this. You couldn't locate a bronze plaque there if your life depended on it.

"Beautiful view," Tony said.

I turned, and there he was beside me, actually using his eyes to apprehend what lay before us. I made no mention of what my colleagues and I would do to this view if given half the chance. "Yes, it is."

A moment of silence passed. I said, "I'm going to Syria."

He didn't reply. He might have thought he misheard me.

"When I get back to Cleveland," I said, "I'm going to Syria. Are you following what's happening in Syria?"

"In Syria? Yes."

"The bombings? The refugees?"

"Yes," he said, nodding and looking off. He was right not to pursue it. What would Syria want with a forty-three-year-old fat man like me?

"Please, take your time," he said, "but I get off now. I meet you there, on other side."

I told him I was ready to go, and we set off together.

"Not my favorite part of Prague, this bridge," he said.

"I thought you said it was the greatest bridge in the world."

"Capitalist boast," he replied.

The remark lingered as we walked past a white-haired accordionist, and in light of it I thought back on other descriptions, other claims. Prague, he had told me as we went along, had the finest architecture, the newest cuisine. The best cars in Europe, the oldest pilsners and pubs. Even what was awful was first in class. The grisliest murders! The bloodiest wars! Everything out of his mouth had been a capitalist boast! I thought I was getting a history lesson, but even history was subject to the prevailing winds, and those winds were currently blowing out of the west.

The bridge marked a difference. On the bridge he went off script for the first time.

"You put to me this question. What was better under Communism than it is today? And to this question, I can only say again: absolutely nothing. But now, in time of capitalism, there are maybe too many tourists in Prague."

"Isn't that good for your business?"

"Yes," he said. "But for the man, maybe not so good."

"What a strange question you put to me," he said a few minutes later. "Most people want to know only horror stories of Communism, but you ask something very different."

We were climbing the stairs to the castle. They were endless, steep, and exhausting, extending at a heavenly grade, and I was winded again. "Let's take a breather," I said.

I reached the ledge and looked out. When had I let the weight go? How had I come to feel so old? When I had the presence of mind again to take in the view, it was of still more gables, dormers, and domes. And in the far distance, cut in half by a rising funicular, a great green swath of civic garden.

"There was very famous Czech TV show called *The Thirty Cases of Major Zeman*," he said. "Have you ever heard of this?"

"No."

"Major Zeman was Communist James Bond. Always bright, tough, and brave, just like Western hero. I am fourteen, fifteen years old, something like this, and we are watching this show every week, me and my father. He was true Communist, believing in socialism, in Soviet Union. Very wonderful man. Now is dead."

"How did he die?"

"Of broken heart," he said, "after Communism ending. We fought about this. We did not see eye to eye. There was nothing better for anyone in Communist times, nothing nothing. But we are watching *Major Zeman* together, and both of us love it. I'm calling him Pavel Danes—Prague Spring reformist character. Always drunk." He smiled. "You make me remember it."

"I watched TV with my dad," I said. "*Crime Story,* with Dennis Farina."

"I think fathers are good at this," he said.

When at last we reached the top of the castle, we were greeted by three armed guards. Antonin exchanged some words in Czech with them.

"They are sending us away," he said. "Something has happened. He doesn't say what."

We returned down the stairs. In Prague, you go from bronze plaque to bronze plaque saying, "Well, thank God that tragedy is over with, at least." Then the next day you learn of the hostage situation: three men, six dead, ties to terrorism. Nothing changes. Catholicism gives way to Protestantism, Communism replaces the church, capitalism effaces Communism, terrorism threatens them all. In my travels since visiting Prague, I've come across other plaques in other cities—London, Warsaw, Montreal—each a single station in a worldwide memorial for the dream of human progress.

"I'm sorry," he said. "That is where we were having our coffee."

The streets unknotted from the historic district, and we left the bridges behind. We entered a new neighborhood, where I saw a sign for a Hooters ("12 Buffalo Wings, 200 Kč") among the stuccoed cherubs and concert halls. A woman called down to someone from a third-floor apartment, and a fat taxi driver, licking a thumb to better turn a tabloid on a stone step, peered up at her, reading glasses perched on the tip of his nose.

"'Killing an Arab,'" Antonin said.

"Sorry?"

"Very famous song by the Cure," he said. "We were at university when we hear this song for first time. We are listening—it is very strange. It changes for us everything. We are starting to dress all in black. Like Robert Smith, you know? At my university, we called this *gotici*."

"*Gotici*," I said.

"If you were *gotik*, like me, you loved the West. We saw *L'Avventura*. We read Philip Roth. This was not acceptable to socialist regime after Prague Spring. We had no choice, we do it behind their backs, and maybe for us that is making it sweeter. Maybe."

I looked over, and saw a man catching up with lost time.

"It was not because of Communism that we love this time. But because we are eighteen, nineteen, twenty. We are young. We are curious. We are free. Strange, I know. But true. Under Communism we are free. And because people are hungry, because they are scared, absolutely nothing is better under Communism. But of course everything is better when you are young."

He smiled. We walked along in silence.

"I'm not listening to music anymore," he said. "I don't know why."

We stood inside the courtyard of a historic palace, now a privately owned boutique hotel. Antonin's voice fell to a whisper. Here Mozart, devastated by the failure of his *Figaro* in Vienna, found refuge in Prague, in the former court of Earl Pachta. "Pachta was great patron for Mozart," Antonin told me, "and in this courtyard, he is making some of his very best music of all time. But now." He gestured. Among the thriving topiary and marble columns of that hotel lobby stood a selection of Škoda cars, on display as in a game show. There was no trace of Mozart. Behind the cars, glossy banners in Czech advertised what any citizen of the world would recognize as technical specifications and fuel efficiencies. Antonin, drawing me closer, loosened the corner of one of the Škoda banners to reveal a plaque that lay concealed beneath, documenting the maestro's presence in this very place and commemorating the composition of his Prague Symphony.

And on Tržiště Street, he stopped me and pointed across the cobblestones.

"Many years ago," he continued, "there was bakery just there. Now it is KFC. But when I was a boy, I was coming to this bakery with my grandmother. Look there, okay, that arch?

When I'm walking with my grandmother, we are going under that arch and up this street, to just there, and the whole street is smelling like fresh baking bread. Was it smelling so good because we are so hungry? Or because I am only six years old? I don't know. But if someone is putting gun to my head and saying you must tell to me the one thing better under Communism, that is what I'm saying to them. The bread," he said. "Smelling the bread. Eating the bread."

We parted outside the Hotel Superior. It was an abrupt farewell—we shook hands, and he was gone.

It was, he told me in parting, for him one of the better tours. He was seeing the city as if for the first time—"in new light," in his words. It was what he loved about Prague, old, familiar Prague: it was never the same city twice. But it also seemed to leave him melancholy. Toward the end, the tour guide had gone quiet.

Like most things in life, after I'd spent all that time bitching and moaning in anticipation, I was sorry it was over. I asked Antonin what I owed him, but he wouldn't take money from me. I watched him dissolve into the foot traffic streaming down Ostrovní, and Prague returned to a place where I was alone, utterly alone.

I retrieved my room key and, surging with feeling, decided to skip the elevator. But something happened to me on the stairs. I was taking them two at a time when I slowed, turned, and abruptly sat down. Overlooking the lobby, I was vaguely aware of a running vacuum and the other rote noises a half-rate hotel makes in the late afternoon. Antonin had been my first history lesson, the only one of any relevance or human scale: history lived inside people's heads as much as it did on plaques or in some formal record. That was bad news for me. In Cleveland, generic-seeming Cleveland, I could not escape a living history of me doing the most horrible things. Pressing myself on women. Telling bald-faced lies. Cheating. Stealing pills from friends' cabinets. Fucking their wives. You'd never believe all the shit I'd done in my life if you were just meeting me in a boardroom, sizing up my suit coat and shaking my hand. Half my life I spent as a monster. I'd done worse, much worse, than pluck a little tulip from the ground. I was no innocent. I was a scourge, a blight, a roving maw. I was a maniac. Fuck my fellow man. I hated him the minute he got in my way. Fuck progress if it meant nothing to me personally. I was a terrible burden and an awful premise, and then I was put into practice, to stain Cleveland and terrorize its citizens. And now I was here, an inheritor of Europe, enjoying a day of sightseeing in beautiful Prague.

If the world had the good fortune of depriving me of vision and an army, that did not mean that I had left anything standing in my little city, from Valley Parkway to Lee Road. They should come for me, I thought. In my way, I merited it just as much as the tyrants.

My reverie ended when I caught sight of the woman from the embassy. What was she doing here, at my hotel? She paused briefly at the front desk before proceeding out the door. I stood, confused. Should I run after her? But what made me think she was here for me? She wouldn't want to see me again. Was she here to see Baxter? But that seemed just as unlikely. It had to be a coincidence of some kind. I returned down the stairs.

"Has someone just left a message for me?" I inquired at the front desk.

No message.

I returned up the stairs and down the hallway to my room.

I found the door unlocked. I pushed it open, slowly, and said, "Hello?" Later I realized that I had been expecting to find someone from housekeeping. But it was the giant—the gloom—who stood, frozen at the sight of me, on the other side of my bed.

We stared at each other.

They're in it together, I thought. I don't know why or how, but they must be. The woman from the embassy and the giant porter. What else explained it?

"What are you doing here?"

"What am *I* doing here?" I said. "What are *you* doing here?"

"No, what are you doing *here,* in Czechoslovakia?"

"Czechoslovakia? What are you doing in my room?"

"I am changing ice bucket," he said.

I looked down at his enormous hands. They were empty. The metal ice bucket was sitting on the table behind him. The window beyond that was open, the curtain fluttering in a light breeze, the whole thing calling to mind the fate of the foreign minister Antonin had told me about that day, a man tossed to his death from an upper-floor balcony. Prague was the defenestration capital of the world. Could the giant lift me off the ground? Could I fit through that window? I felt my legs begin to buckle.

"My ice bucket?" I said, clinging to our conversation. "My ice bucket is there."

I pointed.

"I leave now," he said. But he didn't move.

Was it my place of birth? My normal size? The protections I took for granted as a guest of the hotel? Or was it the impunity I enjoyed from my share of crimes? I will never know what he had in mind when he pointed at me with his long, bony finger and leveled his judgment of unpardonable hate. "You are lucky man," he said. "Very lucky man."

A Fair Price

Nothing sucked more than moving your stuff out of storage. Luckily Jack had a hand. Guy he'd never met before named Mike. Ryan, his yard guy, had hooked them up. Mike worked for Ryan or knew Ryan somehow. Jack didn't ask. He was just glad to have the help. He did hope this Mike was more efficient than Ryan. Ryan—what a talker.

Mike pulled up to the gate at the top of the hill and honked. Jack went over to the gooseneck post and keyed the code in, and the gate began to retract. Mike was twenty bucks an hour. A fair price. Worth every penny, too. But one more reason to hope he was efficient.

Jack allowed his gaze to wander as Mike came toward him down the blacktop path. Boring place, the U-Stor-It. Ugly. The whole thing a chore.

Totally reasonable, as Mike approached, to expect him to slow up, roll the window down, and introduce himself, shake hands, etc., before parking. But no, Mike blew right past.

Well, all right. Fair enough. Jack undraped his arm from the post and followed after.

When he reached the rental unit, Jack expected Mike to hop out so the two of them could get down to business. But Mike idled behind tinted windows for the next ten minutes. Texting a buddy in there, or updating a profile. Who knows what. Well, you couldn't expect a younger man to have the same manners and priorities as a man of forty-two.

But when he finally stepped foot from his pickup, Mike wasn't a young man after all. Had to be fifty, at least. Paint-spattered work boots and a puffed-up face. Prickly sort of man—that was the impression, anyway. The neighbors would know to steer clear. The croissant and latte Jack had bought him that morning as a gesture of kindness seemed wrong now, real wrong, and would unfortunately go to waste.

"Hey, you Mike?"

Mike replied with a single nod. He fixed a can of chewing tobacco between his tiny teeth as he screwed on a Yankees cap and flicked the door shut. Didn't say Jack's name in return. Not there for names. There for a simple exchange: labor for cash.

And that was okay. They could get straight to work that way.

"Thanks for coming on such short notice, Mike. Did Ryan tell you what we're up to today?"

"Said you needed a hand moving," Mike said.

"I need to clear everything out of here and take it all down to Red Hook," Jack said. "Moving in with my fiancée. We're getting married in June. You married? No, you'd be wearing a ring. Then again, not everybody wears a ring these days. Lisa and I have been talking nothing but rings lately. Anyway, this friend of ours owns a vineyard in Livingston, looks out over the Hudson. Beautiful place. And he offered it to us, so why not? Hayrides for the kids afterward. And there'll be dancing, of course. Getting a nice big tent for that."

Mike nodded once at the mention of Livingston and turned away again.

"Anyway," Jack continued, "this unit is a relic of the old life. I need it emptied out, need all my stuff in one place, need to be done paying the monthly fee. It's sixty-nine bucks a month—adds up, you know? Every little bit counts these days. Nice people, though. In the front office, I mean. If you ever need a storage unit in the area, I'd recommend it. Anyway," he said.

When Mike made no reply to any of this, Jack knew the man hated him. It was only an intuition, but it went bone deep. Mike had driven right past him when he should have stopped and introduced himself, and then made him wait ten minutes in the cold while he texted or whatever. A man like Mike would be terrible to Jack if given half the chance. He wouldn't let Jack stop to relieve himself on a long car ride. He'd stop only to fill up on gas, saying to Jack, "If you're not out here by the time I'm done, I will leave you." And he wasn't joking. Jack would run to and from the men's room in terror.

Mike turned and looked at Jack for the first time. He had startlingly wet, beautiful blue eyes. "Did Ryan tell you how much I charge?"

"He said twenty an hour."

Mike nodded. "Twenty's my hourly rate."

"I couldn't do it without you, Mike, obviously, so to me twenty's a steal. I'm sure you have better things to do with your time on a Sunday morning."

"Twenty's my hourly rate," Mike repeated.

"Twenty it is, then," said Jack. "Shall we get started?"

Jack raised the gate on the rental unit, and he and Mike sized up its contents. He was reminded of just how many boxes there were, how much crap he owned. He had a fantasy of leaving it all behind.

"Well, what do you think, Mike?" he said. "How should we do this?"

"I think we just start moving it," Mike said.

He took two steps forward, picked a pair of boxes off the nearest stack, and strode up the ramp with them as if storming a castle. Before Jack could take hold of a box of his own, Mike was on his way back down again.

You couldn't win. If you said, "Let's plan this out so we do it right," a man like Mike looked at you like you were an idiot. "It ain't brain science, boy," he'd say, and then he'd just go at it. But if you said nothing of the kind, if you just went at it yourself, a man like Mike would stop you right away. "Whoa, whoa, whoa! Don't be a fucking retard. You can't just willy-nilly start throwing shit in when you're moving a big load. Are you no brighter than a fucking lamppost?"

Jack picked up two boxes of his own and headed after Mike in a hurry, but midway up the ramp he lost his balance. To steady himself he had to let the top box go as it began to slide off. A few things went through his mind before it even hit the ground. Clumsy. Not up to the task. Never send a boy to do a man's job. But when he looked back, Mike wasn't even paying attention. He carried on into the van.

Mike came up behind him in no time with two more boxes.

"Sorry," Jack said, hurrying to get out of the bigger man's way.

He retrieved the box that fell, and Mike headed to the storage unit for two more boxes. They met up again seconds later, Mike now at six boxes to Jack's two.

Why was he keeping score like that? It wasn't a competition. And if Mike thought it was? Well, he'd hired Mike. If he wanted to, he could sit back and make Mike do all the work.

They worked in silence to start with, but soon Jack made an attempt at some friendly conversation. The weather, and what a pain in the ass it was to move.

"You live around here, Mike?" he asked.

"What?"

"Oh, I was just asking...do you live around here?"

They were coming down the dull metal ramp, Jack first, his head thrown back. He thought he saw Mike nod. But he offered no further detail, and Jack didn't pursue the matter. Some guys had a scruple about their privacy. And who could blame them? Mike might have taken a dislike for whatever reason, but Jack appreciated a man who didn't feel the need to talk all the time.

But could you imagine offering a man like that a latte and a croissant? There was no way! He shook his head at himself.

He caught up with Mike a few seconds later. "So you're a Yankees fan, huh?"

"Huh?"

"Yankees fan?"

Jack gestured at the hat on Mike's head. Mike removed it, looked at it cockeyed, and put it back on. Then he picked up two more boxes and took them into the van.

The two men soon hit upon a rhythm. Jack picked up two boxes, walked them into the van, and returned down the ramp just as Mike was heading up the ramp with two boxes of his own. Then Mike came down the ramp as Jack was going up it, and on they went like that, back and forth, up and down, real companionable for twenty minutes.

"Oh, hey, Mike, I almost forgot," he said when Mike was still in the van. "I picked up a pastry for you. If you're hungry. It's in the cab of the truck. It's from Le Perche."

Well, why not? Stupid just to let it go to waste. And stupid not to follow through on a gesture of kindness just because Mike had a mean-looking face.

Mike came forward, pulling chewing tobacco from the can. Jack didn't see how such a fat wad was going to fit inside Mike's small, angry mouth, but Mike deposited it with a weird elegance, and it disappeared completely behind a lip. He wiped a glistening brown fingertip on his jeans and screwed the lid back on. "From where?" he asked. He spat to the ground.

"Oh," Jack said. "From Le Perche? You know it? The French place on Warren? With the good pastries?"

Mike looked at him. "French place," he said.

He wiped his mouth with the back of his hand, jumped down to the pavement, and that was that. He carried on to the unit and went ahead by two more boxes.

*　　*　　*

What was only intuition a moment ago now seemed obvious. Mike hated him. It was strange. With an unreasonable hatred like Mike's, you almost feared for your life. Not that he'd bash Jack's head in with a table lamp for being annoying or for making the same mistake over and over again. But he'd certainly sooner watch him die than show him any kindness or respect.

Well, if that was how he wanted it, and if he couldn't say thanks or keep up his end of a little conversation, Jack would just stay silent, too. Why make any more effort trying to befriend him or reassure him? You couldn't reassure a man like Mike, not of your competence or your kindness or your membership in the fraternity of men. You just had to go about your business, keeping your guard up, and part ways as soon as possible, to protect yourself. What better way to do that than by keeping silent? Jack vowed not to say another word unless and until Mike said something first.

"I'm sorry about all these boxes," Jack said the next pass up the ramp.

Mike just shrugged. What did he care? It was twenty bucks an hour for him either way.

Mike had the misfortune of resembling Donnie. The thing was, just very recently Donnie had turned sentimental. Didn't understand why Jack wasn't inviting him to his wedding. "Then your mother's not going, either, then, forget it," Donnie told him over the phone. It was just like Donnie to be on the line when Jack was trying to talk to his mom. Well, okay, fine, stay home, both of you. It wasn't like his mom was some great hero. What had she ever done to keep Donnie in check when he was a kid?

But Lisa's complaint was: If you don't invite anybody from your family, who's going to be sitting on your side of the aisle? We can't have a wedding where all the guests are on one side.

Like the wedding was some kind of boat and it would capsize if Jack didn't invite every single person he'd ever known.

"I'm not saying you have to invite every single person you've ever known," Lisa said whenever the topic came up. "I'm just saying, why not let bygones be bygones?"

Well, a wedding wasn't a boat, was it? He wasn't going to invite Donnie just to put butts in seats.

But this guy Mike wasn't Donnie. Mike was a friend or an associate of Ryan's, out here in the cold on a Sunday morning for a measly twenty bucks an hour. Jack didn't hate *him*. To be honest, he felt sorry for the guy. Must fucking suck to be so old and still be making your living with your back.

"Give me a hand with this, Mike, will you?"

Mike looked at the leather sofa Jack had taken hold of. "You want that in the van now?"

"Let's just get it over with," Jack said.

"Okay," he said, squatting low. "Your call."

A man like Mike usually had some kind of nickname. Jack couldn't say just what it would be. He thought it might come out at the wedding. "Call me Griff," Mike would say. Both men would have knocked back more than a few by then. "We sure had fun moving all that stuff of yours down to Red Hook, didn't we, Jack?" There was nothing like a day of manual labor to forge a bond between two guys. "Hey, and by the way.

Thanks for inviting me. I'm real honored." Lisa would have to pull him away. "I do love how easily you make new friends," she'd say. He'd circle back before the night was through and part from Griff with a hug. Griff turning to his date afterward, saying, "Love that guy."

So it didn't work out that way. So what? It had always been a long shot.

Once Mike warmed up, he started to spurn the ramp. With a load in hand he leapt from the blacktop to the metal bumper and into the van. He wrangled extension cords like a ranch hand. And even when you thought a load was too heavy and his hands were all full, on his way out he reached for a standing lamp and took that, too. He was impressive. But it was laughable just how little he said.

When Jack brought in his next load, he found Mike in there talking on the phone. Turned away, muttering low, filling the back of the van completely, so that Jack was forced to go around him.

So he did talk, just not to Jack.

Jack wouldn't have minded talking on the phone. One more conversation with Lisa about the goddamn invite list would have been preferable to moving boxes out of storage and into a moving van.

He took out his cell phone. How was Mike getting service? Discount carrier, probably. They had weird coverage. Oh, well. Jack put his phone away and returned to the unit.

He dropped off another load and went back for more. He made a second trip and then another. Mike was on the phone that whole time.

Well, you know what? People call, they need your help,

nobody can time an emergency. All Jack needed was a little gesture. "Sorry about this," Mike might have whispered while cupping the mouthpiece. "Off in a minute."

But another five minutes went by, and still no such gesture. He had even taken a seat on one of the boxes in there!

Once you disdain someone, once you decide they're not worth your respect, you do whatever you damn well please, even if he's paying you twenty bucks an hour.

"It's 27–24, just so you know," Jack said to him.

Mike looked up from his call. "What's that?"

"Oh, I was just saying that I've brought in twenty-seven boxes to your twenty-four."

Mike's dark monobrow furrowed. "You're keeping score?"

Jack left the van. Yeah, like Mike hadn't been keeping score, too, until he found it more important to talk on the damn phone.

He expected an apology when Mike got off at last, but Mike didn't offer one. He simply came down the ramp and carried a new load into the van.

What are we here for? Jack wondered. The question had started running through his mind before Mike was even off the phone. What are we here for? It obviously wasn't mutual respect. It wasn't to make new friends. So what was it? Was it just lifting and moving things in exchange for cash? Was that it? Squatting and lifting and climbing and digging and kneeling and hammering things in for a payday and nothing more?

"What are we here for, Mike?" he found himself asking out loud.

Not gonna go over well. But you know what? Fuck it. What did he have to lose?

Bent over, Mike looked up at him with one squinting blue eye. You could practically smell the fumes pouring off him from last night's bender.

"Is it just to move things? Or do we have some greater purpose in life? I like to think we're here for something greater. As men, I mean. But that's my two cents. What do you think? Think it's possible that you and I—"

Mike let out a terrific groan as he lifted the oversized AC unit flush off the cement floor and began to crab-walk it toward the van.

It wasn't until Jack happened upon an open box of old photographs that he began to rethink everything. Here was a shot of his Uncle Vern wearing several strands of Mardi Gras beads, puckering up before a silver trumpet. Uncle Vern would have been invited to the wedding were he still alive. And here was a rare one of his dad, also dead. His buddy Horvath—lost track of that guy after leaving Denver. Here was one of Steve and what's-her-name. She never cared for Jack, and when Steve married her, that was the end of his friendship with Steve. And here was a little photo album in among the loose pictures documenting his tortured years with Sandra. Obviously couldn't invite her. Here was one of Donnie: wide grin, cigar in his mouth, holding a fish in each hand on some dock, that stupid gap between his two front teeth. He couldn't invite him, he just couldn't. Or any of them. Take your pick. Except for Aunt Julia. But she had sent her regrets.

He tossed the box aside. Add it to the rest of the heap and let it burn.

"Be right back, Mike," he said as he left the van.

He walked up the blacktop path, past the office (deserted on Sundays), to County Route 9. Service was less spotty up there. He paced near the busy road as cars washed by until Lisa picked up. He could tell she'd been crying.

"What is it?" he asked. But he knew. "The invite list?"

"I'm sorry, Jack," she said. "I can't help it."

"Fuck it," he said. "Invite 'em. Whoever you want, invite 'em."

She caught her breath. "Do you mean it?"

"Yeah, I mean it," he said. "What do I care? I just want you to be happy."

"Oh, Jack," she said. She hadn't sounded so happy in weeks. "What a relief!" She let out a big sigh. "Donnie, too?"

"Whoever," he said. "What do I care? You can finally meet the bastard. Might be nice, actually. He'll ask your niece for a blow job, and your mother will finally understand why I never bring family around."

"Jenny's eleven, Jack."

"I'm just trying to prepare you."

"Let's not talk about my niece, okay?"

"Okay."

"Oh, Jack," she said, "thank you. This means so much to me. You have no idea."

"What else are we here for, right, Leese?"

"I love you, Jackie. You're such a good man."

"Love you too, Leese."

He hung up and went happily down the hill.

*　　*　　*

"You got a problem," Mike said when he returned.

"What is it?"

"Come see."

"Comme ça."

"What?"

"Never mind."

They had run out of room in the back of the van. But that wasn't Jack's fault! That was Mike's fault! He was the one who had failed to make a plan!

"Told you it was too early to put that sofa in," Mike said.

"Oh, so this is my fault?"

Mike shrugged.

A minute passed. Mike took a seat on a box as if he were inside the van talking on the phone again.

But he was right. They were out of room. They could either push on, or they could take the sofa out and start over, as Donnie would have insisted he do. "And do it right this time," he'd have said, giving Jack a slap upside the head.

"Well, what are we doing? It's getting cold."

"Let's take the fucking thing out," Jack said.

Donnie had been right a lot of the time—that was the trouble. Jack had to admit it. Donnie did things properly. He knew a thing or two. Jack had known very little. Of course, Jack had been ten years old or whatever. He couldn't do things as Donnie wanted them done, as a grown man did them. But now Jack was forty-two years old, and he was still making a hash of things. There were boxes on the ground; there were boxes in the van; there were boxes in the unit.

Maybe his age had had nothing to do with it. Maybe Donnie

was right about that, too. Making a hash of things was just Jack's nature.

They were relaying the last of the book boxes from the van to the ground before taking the sofa out.

"How about I pay you in books, Mike?" he said. "God knows I got enough of them."

Mike handed off a box and went back for another.

"Not twenty *bucks* an hour but twenty *books* an hour," he said. It was something Donnie would have said, but he wasn't serious like Donnie. He was just playing around. "What do you say? Will you take your day's pay in books?"

He went back for another box, but Mike met him at the edge of the van empty handed. He stared down at Jack, and the look on his face said it all.

"It was just a joke," Jack said.

"Twenty's my hourly rate," Mike said.

"I know," he said. "I was just joking."

But now in his mind the question had been raised, and Jack realized that Mike's view of things was the only correct one from the start. This was a simple exchange, labor for cash. It had nothing to do with gestures of kindness, or if you knew the other guy's name or not, or what man's ultimate purpose on earth might be. What the market would bear—that was the only relevant question.

So, was twenty really a fair price?

The answer was no. And not because Mike disdained Jack from the start, or wasted all that time talking on the phone, or took a seat whenever he felt like it. These days, there was bound to be someone willing to work for less—for fifteen an hour, even ten—and to toss in a bit of humanity for free.

The matter was settled long ago, but negotiations could always be reopened. "Look, Mike," he might have said, "you and I both know that in today's job market, I don't have to pay twenty bucks an hour to find unskilled manual labor. So here's what we're going to do." He'd hand over what was owed to Mike, saying fair's fair. "But if you want the full job, I'm afraid it's fifteen an hour from here on out." What would the big man say to that? Would that get him talking?

"Hey, Mike," he said.

Was he really going to do it? They had removed the sofa from the van and were loading things back in.

"What did we say, twenty an hour?"

Mike stopped what he was doing and straightened up. "Yeah?"

"Because I've been thinking more about it."

"What about?"

"Well, like how you were in there for a while talking on the phone."

More displeasure from Mike's monobrow. "Yeah?"

"Is twenty really fair?"

Suddenly Jack felt like an asshole, like Donnie. Donnie did shit like that, not Jack. Mike, poor Mike, out here on a Sunday in the cold, getting yanked around! And for what? For nothing more than reminding Jack of Donnie. And in the meantime, look what it was doing to Jack. It was turning him into Donnie!

Boom, boom, boom. Mike was down the ramp in no time. What, was he going to beat the shit out of him? "I told you already," he said. "I don't do nothing for less than twenty."

"Yeah, but Mike. It's just moving shit."

Mike, agitated, cocked his head. Jack had said the wrong thing.

"How's twenty-five?" Jack said suddenly.

"What?"

"I said how's twenty-five?"

"Are you fucking with me?" Mike asked. "I thought we agreed to twenty."

"And now I'm offering you more."

"How come?"

"Oh, just take it, Mike. You're out here in the cold on a Sunday morning. Take it."

Jack went around him and up the ramp. He was glad to put some distance between them. The look on Mike's face had been pure murder.

Not worth twenty, and now suddenly he was paying him twenty-five. Over and over again he'd been told to keep his fucking mouth shut, but did he ever listen? No, and now look at what you've gone and done.

Even after reorganizing the van, there wasn't enough room for all of Jack's things. They were going to have to make two trips after all. Jack shuttered the gate and joined Mike in the cab.

Mike had his boot up on the dash and was eating the croissant from Le Perche. Jack stared at him in open disbelief. "What are you doing?"

"What?"

"You didn't want that."

"Yeah, I did."

"You sure didn't acknowledge it."

"Acknowledge it?"

"Yeah, you didn't acknowledge it. You didn't say thanks. You didn't say anything. Would it have killed you to say thanks when I offered it to you?"

"Thanks," Mike said.

"What are you, a fucking retard?"

It just came out. Mike stared at Jack as he pointedly dropped what remained of the croissant, crumpled the bag up while chewing, and tossed it to the floor of the van.

Jack put the van in gear. They went like a cloud over the fresh blacktop, through the gate and out of the valley to County Route 9.

They passed the rock quarry on the left, the gray pyramids of limestone and granite, and the iced-over pond in the distance, cowlicked with reeds. The road was stained white with salt from a long winter. Jack glanced over at Mike, who was now staring out the passenger-side window as if dreaming on his way back to the penitentiary. He wasn't going to say a word. All the way down to Red Hook and all the way back, not a fucking word. A man could do that, a man could choose not to speak. Be a man like Mike and shut up. Will you just shut the fuck up? Shut up now or God help me I will shut you up.

"You never asked my name," Jack said.

He waited for a reply. When none came, he said:

"This morning, when we met. You didn't ask, and I didn't offer. You remember?"

"You know, you talk too much," Mike said.

"Is that right?"

"Yeah, that is right. We'd have been done a lot sooner if you talked a little less."

"That's interesting," Jack said.

More silence. Then:

"You curious?"

"Huh?"

"I said, 'Are you curious?'"

"About what?"

"What my name is."

"Oh. Well, Ryan told it to me."

"Did he?"

"Yeah."

"So you know it, then."

"Yeah."

Dull brown fields extended for acres. Then the road narrowed and shade trees crowded the shoulders. In clearings swiftly opened and swiftly shut again, modest ranch houses flitted by. Then the broad fields returned.

"What is it?" Jack asked.

"Huh?"

"What's my name?"

Mike stared straight ahead.

"You don't know it, do you?"

"Ryan did tell it to me," he said finally. "I must of forgot it."

Jack was silent.

"I believe it might be Jack," Mike said. "Is that it?"

Jack didn't answer. They turned down a private drive lined with tall trees. They climbed a slow, meandering hill to a restored farmhouse with a view of the mountains, where they unloaded without a word. A lovely porch, a tree swing, a cherrywood canoe beside the artificial pond. He had everything in the world he'd ever wanted. Stupid to let Mike get under his skin like that.

"What do you think, Mike?"

"About what?"

"About this view."

"Asshole," Mike muttered.

The two men got back in the van. The miles rolled by, and the silence intensified.

"I talk too much?" Jack said.

"I think so," Mike said.

"Well, you talk too little."

"Is that right?"

"Would it kill you to carry on a little conversation?"

Mike made no reply.

Halfway to the storage facility, Jack pulled off to the shoulder. "You drive," he said.

"What for?"

He opened the door, and the sounds of the world rushed in. He went around the van and opened the door on Mike's side.

"What am I driving for?"

"Because I'm paying you."

Mike moved over, and Jack got in. Mike pulled out amid the traffic heading north.

"But not twenty-five dollars an hour, Mike," Jack announced on the straightaway. "I'm not paying you that."

Mike looked over. "You told me you would," he said.

"I told you twenty. Then I got to joking around, and this other thing came out, I don't know why. I made a mistake, and I apologize for it. But twenty-five's too much."

"You're paying me the twenty-five," Mike said.

"I don't think I am."

"I think you are."

Mike went through the light at the junction and turned into the storage facility. Jack got out at the gate and punched in the code, then slipped through the fence while Mike had to wait for it to retract. A minute later Mike blew past him. When Jack arrived at the rental unit, the bigger man was not in the cab texting, as he had been earlier in the day, but pacing back and forth on the blacktop, his breath visible in the cold. He came to a sudden stop and said, "I ain't helping you with the rest."

"Oh yes you are."

"Something's wrong with you," Mike said.

"Something's wrong with me?"

"I want what you owe me. And I want twenty-five an hour for it, just like you promised."

"You know what I used to be told, Mike? Stop acting all high and mighty, that's what I used to be told, and get the *fuck* back to work."

Every time Donnie came forward, as Mike did now, Jack called social services, but nothing ever changed. Well, this time Jack swung first, aiming for Mike's throat.

Mike looked silly going down. "You look like a little girl!" Mike would have said to him had the tables been turned. But no, Mike looked more like a big fat eleven-year-old boy, a bully easily stunned and not likely to fight back when you stood up to him once and for all. Jack was surprised. Mike gripped his throat on the way down and began to gasp for air.

Had the tables been turned, Mike would have told Jack to

get up, get the fuck up you little pussy, but Jack didn't want Mike up. He had put on a pair of steel-toed boots that morning to protect his feet during the move, and now he walked around Mike, timing every kick with a question.

"You drive past me? You don't introduce yourself? You make me wait in the cold while you text? You talk on the phone for ten minutes, but to me you can't say a word? You eat my croissant and you don't say thanks? You don't know my fucking *name?*"

He grew short of breath and had to stop kicking. He bent over, resting his elbows on his knees.

Mike was still clutching his windpipe. He made a sucking sound as he tried to take in air. There was blood on the blacktop.

"All right, get up," he said to Mike. "Come on now, get up."

Jack nudged him. Then he sat next to him on the pavement. The traffic was washing faintly past, high up on County Route 9.

"All right, I'll pay you," Jack said. "I'll pay you the twenty-five. Okay?"

Jack bent down close to listen for an answer, but all he heard was the struggle for air. That was hard to believe. Mike was such a strong man, much stronger than he was.

He should have started without him. If only he'd taken a few boxes into the van while Mike was in there texting, he might not have fallen behind in the count, and then none of this would have happened.

"I was even considering inviting you to my wedding," he said.

Didn't matter now. Pretty much all that mattered was what

Jack would do next. He had options he'd never dreamed of having when he was under Donnie's thumb. He could say to Mike, as had so often been said to him, "You have only yourself to blame," and leave him there, struggling to breathe in that desolate storage facility, so as to teach him a lesson. Or he could man up, as he had fantasized the men of the world would do when he was a boy and at their mercy. Mike was turning blue. He needed to see a doctor. Jack was a good man, but now he had to ask himself a serious question. What does a man do— and I mean a real man, now, what does a real man do—when he knows he's done something wrong?

Acknowledgments

My thanks to Willing Davidson and his colleagues at *The New Yorker* for working with me on several of these stories and improving them with great sensitivity and insight. Willing is sharp, fierce, and bullshit proof, which makes his enthusiasm (when it comes) all the more meaningful.

Thanks to my early readers, always steadfast and encouraging: Robert Howell, Daniel Kraus, Christopher Mickus, David Morse, Grant Rosenberg, and especially Matthew Thomas, whose bright scalpel mind cuts to the heart of the matter every time.

Thanks to the editors of the magazines, journals, and books where these stories appeared: Amie Barrodale, Natalie Danford, John Kulka, Heidi Pitlor, Kathy Poires and Rob Spillman, and to the folks at *Prairie Schooner* and the *Iowa Review*. A special thanks to David Hamilton.

I'm also very grateful to Jennifer Egan, Jennifer Haigh, Edward Jones, Francine Prose, and Richard Russo for having championed individual stories included in this collection.

There would be no collection as a whole without two editors in particular: Reagan Arthur at Little, Brown and Mary Mount at Viking. The final purpose of writing is to commune with readers like you, and I have reason to thank you both every day. The same goes for Georg Reuchlein at Random House.

Acknowledgments

Finally, a special thanks to two women, my agent, Julie Barer, and my wife, Eliza Kennedy, who never make the mistake of confusing the author for his (awful, male) characters, and who in turn embolden the author to make those characters more male and awful still.

And here's to the old man, who's missed.

About the Author

Joshua Ferris was born in 1974 in Danville, Illinois. His first novel, *Then We Came to the End,* was published in 2007 to wide acclaim. Translated into more than thirty languages, it won the PEN/Hemingway Award and the Barnes and Noble Discover Award and was shortlisted for the National Book Award. His second novel, *The Unnamed,* was published in 2011. In 2014, his third novel, *To Rise Again at a Decent Hour,* was shortlisted for the Man Booker Prize and won the biannual International Dylan Thomas Prize. Ferris was named by *The New Yorker* one of the best "20 Under 40" writers in 2010. He lives in Hudson, New York, with his wife and son.